Milagros

Tess Almendárez Lojacono

Laughing Cactus Press
Imprint of Silver Boomer Books
Abilene, Texas
www.LaughingCactusPress.com

Published by Laughing Cactus Press,
Imprint of Silver Boomer Books,
3301 S 14th Suite 16 - PMB 134, Abilene Texas 79605

Cover copyright © 2011 Silver Boomer Books
MILAGROS, Copyright © 2011 by Tess Almendárez
    Lojacono
Cover image of milagro copyright © 2011 Reign Trading
    Company, www.MexicanSugarSkull.com
Published by Laughing Cactus Press,
Imprint of Silver Boomer Books
Abilene, Texas
www.LaughingCactusPress.com
www.SilverBoomerBooks.com
ISBN: 978-0-9826243-4-0

Printed in the United States of America

"I love you without knowing how,
or when, or from where.
I love you straightforwardly,
without complexities or pride;
so I love you
because I know no other way."

Pablo Neruda

This story is dedicated to my
beloved husband Frank,
who said to me one day,
"You should write a book."

Table of Contents

Heaven Is

Claudio stood in the doorway watching his daughter, oblivious now to the worn, bunched carpet, low windows, paint peeling from their sills, the chipped bureau his wife had rescued from someone else's garbage. Mercedes was kneeling by her bed, intent upon a project.

"Hey." His voice, a golden thread, drifted into the room. "What are you doing?"

She didn't turn. "Drawing," came the grave reply.

He moved closer and looked over her shoulder. A piece of cardboard was balanced on the bed's flowered comforter. She was using markers. Her mother didn't allow markers upstairs, in the bedroom, but he wouldn't say anything. The cardboard was divided into three parts.

He perched on the edge of the bed, careful not to jostle the artist or her work. "What is it?"

Mercedes stopped for a moment, tilted her head. "I'm studying on heaven – on getting to heaven." She resumed drawing.

"You mean, like what you have to do?"

"No."

"You mean like, a map of how to get there?"

"No."

They were quiet for a while. Claudio studied the cardboard. In the first section was a picture of blue bird eggs, resting in their nest, a baby bottle like the one Mercedes had clung to for years, a pink blanket and what looked like a drawing of a mother holding a little girl; Mercedes and her mom, no doubt. In the middle section was a picture of a foal, cut from a magazine, a pizza, a purple house, and the photo of Mercedes' mother she kept in her backpack to look at when she was feeling sad at school. The last section showed a prayer book and a rosary draped over a golden chalice and a cross, surrounded by a field of orange flowers. Mercedes finished coloring in a crown, just above the cross. She sat back on her heels.

"See," she pointed to the blue eggs. "This is the beginning. On earth. Next, comes life. Regular stuff, you know? Stuff you love like houses and pets and toys – ooh! Toys!" She grabbed a green marker and began adding a teddy bear. While she drew she hummed. Finished, she rocked back up on her knees and murmured, "And then there's heaven." She added a little more yellow to the crown. "It's like a chart."

"It's a great chart." Her father's eyes filled.

"Daddy, is heaven the same for everyone?"

"I don't know."

She blinked, surprised. "Oh."

"I don't know if it's even what we think it is. You remember what your mother always said, 'God knows best.'" Mercedes nodded. He gathered her onto his lap. She was taller than he realized. Her feet almost touched the floor.

"Put your heaven on the chart, Daddy."

Claudio leaned over her and lifted the photo of his wife. He kissed it once and laid it in the section that was heaven.

Claudio was remembering a conversation he had with his Adelina long ago, when they were first married and expecting Mercedes.

"Poor, poor Lourdes! I know there's something wrong!"

He laughed. "Adela! You're always worrying about others. Lourdes has had three children already. Why would anything be wrong with this one?"

Adela frowned. "It's not me. She told me this one feels different. We'll just have to pray for her and the baby. God knows best."

It turned out Adela was right. This one was different. No sooner was the tiny creature born than she was given a death sentence. Leukemia. Lourdes was out of her mind with grief.

"Claudio," Adela had pleaded when Mercedes was delivered, healthy, brown and round, "Lourdes is going to lose her faith. I know it!"

"Now, Adelina, didn't you say yourself, 'God knows best'? He'll take care of her."

"Yes, yes." She bit her lip and then, as if hurrying would make it hurt less, she plunged ahead. "He must be the one who gave me the idea, then. I couldn't have thought it up all by myself." She stood over the bassinet. "We can't know the depth of her grief, but Claudio, Lourdes

is a convert. Her belief is not that strong, not
yet. If she loses Nuria she will lose her faith as
well. It will be two deaths, not one. And how will
she get into heaven? And here we are with a
healthy baby and a strong faith and..."

"You cannot be suggesting that we give our
precious baby to Lourdes! You cannot even be
thinking that she, that I..."

Adela put her hands on her husband's shoulders. They were the same height exactly. She
loved the way she could look straight into
Claudio's eyes, without even getting on her toes.
"Claudio," she said steadily. "I'm not talking
about giving our child to Lourdes."

"Then, what?"

"To God."

"What?"

"Claudio, what if God takes our child instead?
What if we ask Him to welcome our Mercedes
into His kingdom instead of taking little Nuria?"
Claudio was stunned into silence. "She would go
straight to heaven! Lourdes would keep her baby
and her faith and..."

"But she has three other children! She has a
husband! She can have more! And you – we..."

Adela put her hand over his mouth, gently,
gently. "Yes, yes. We have only one. But we will
have more as well, no?"

"No! I mean, I don't know, but I do know
I will never agree to such a thing!" He had
stamped and fumed and nearly hit his precious
wife. "What kind of a God do you think He is,
that He would make such a bargain with you?"

Claudio's anger was her proof that he believed God would do just as she suggested, that He would sacrifice an innocent life to save the souls of others. She loved Claudio's faith, his devotion to God and to her and their new family. She would not ask again. "You are right, doubtless. I was only looking for a solution. God knows best." She picked up the baby and fed her, though it was not yet time.

Claudio passed his hand over his eyes. That was so long ago. What kind of God, indeed. Nuria had died at three. Lourdes had left the church. Now Adela was gone too. What would he have done without his Mercedes? Perhaps God really did know best. He pressed his face into her hair.

"Daddy, are you crying?"

"No, Love. Only thinking."

"Grandma says we have to go to purgatory before we can get into heaven, but I don't know what that looks like. Do you, Daddy?"

He smiled wistfully. "No one knows what purgatory looks like, though some of us may know a little, how it will feel."

"How, Daddy?"

"Oh," he stroked her hair. "That too, may be different for everyone. But don't worry. Whatever it is, we can bear it because we know it means heaven's just around the corner."

Your Unfailing All-knowing Love

Mamá was mixing bread dough by the kitchen window, pressing and pulling in a culinary tug of war. It took all her strength to mix four loaves at once, flour up to her elbows, tendrils of hair escaping from her bun, but it hardly made sense to do less. Her good bread disappeared as fast as she made it. Why, her family could hammer away a whole loaf in one sitting. Mamá smiled, then crossed herself against the sin of pride.

Modesta was always saying, "That's too much work! Why not just buy a loaf at the store?"

Those sickly soft things they call bread? Mamá snorted as she slapped her dough. It was a sin to call such cotton *bread*! Her bread could stand up to thick bacon sandwiches and homemade blackberry jam. Hers melted in your mouth like cake. Indeed, after supper Father often buttered a big slice for dessert.

At the thought of her husband, Mamá crossed herself again, this time not for pride, but for love. Everything she did was done for him. She meant to work for God, to make her life a prayer, but since the first time she saw Manuel, long before they were married, his was the face she pictured as she wiped her brow, bent her back to the task at hand. She shrugged. Perhaps her daughters would do better...

Mamá tried to teach her girls the beauty of the old ways, though in these modern times it was hard. She paused to listen to a cardinal, her Adelina's favorite. It brought to mind the house-keeping lessons she taught many summers ago, beginning outdoors, with the wash.

Mamá was taking the sheets from the line, folding them and dropping them neatly into a large plastic basket and wondering once again why the stores would insist on selling plastic instead of the beautiful wicker that she used as a girl. Things were so slick, so convenient now; they took all the romance out of life. She pressed a pillowcase to her face and inhaled. Ah, the sweet smell of sunshine and soap remained the same as ever. "Girls," she instructed, "take a pillowcase and smell it. There's your proof that the old ways are the best."

Adela and Modesta stood waiting under the old buckeye tree, arms crossed, mouths stretched into grimaces of disdain. Each strolled over and buried her nose as instructed. Modesta immediately drew back, smoothing an eyebrow. "Yes, yes, very nice, but I never notice the smell when I go to bed at night."

"You don't?" Adela said, then "Ow!" when Modesta hit her with a clothespin.

"I just don't see why you have to use the line," Modesta whined. "It's so much more work than the dryer. And a wringer washer? When the new Kenmores are..."

Mamá picked up the full basket. "I will not throw my family's clothing into a box where I cannot even see whether it is getting clean. You are not washing at all, but letting a machine do your work and just keeping your fingers crossed that it does a good job! No control, no responsibility."

"Mamá," Adela had gently protested, "laundry is a chore, not a duty."

"Ah," Mamá made both girls look away with her piercing gaze, "that is the problem with the world, girls. Until everything you do becomes duty, you will never find your purpose." Mamá turned to walk down the hill to the house. "Time to wring out that last load. And stop rolling your eyes, Modesta."

Adela laughed, skipping after her mother. "Mamá, show me again how you use the wringer without getting your arm caught. And what do you do when the blue jeans get wound around the roller?"

The girls had spent that whole day doing laundry with Mamá, washing and hanging the clothes, sheets, even the towels. Of course, now Mamá hung only the sheets, succumbing finally to the ease of the dryer for the rest. She wondered whether Modesta had ever really understood those lessons. Adela had. She'd hung her wash out every week, even in winter, so fully had she grasped her mother's meaning. Until she became too weak to do the work herself, then Mamá helped Claudio to do it.

Claudio had never questioned what his wife wanted. He didn't tell her to use the dryer. He was grateful that she preferred a simple life, one that he could provide. He sensed a quiet strength behind her desires, a clean no-nonsense direction, as if all her decisions were handed to her from a higher source. She remained steadfast always. He had loved that, too.

Mamá went to look for the birdseed. "Carlitos forgot to put it out again," she murmured. She finished filling the feeder then arched her back and stretched, lifting her arms. The scent of cut grass mixed with the fragrance from the petunias around the patio. Mamá smiled. She considered petunias a homely flower, but their fragrance was delicious. She laughed at the cat, chasing a grasshopper. Oh, Adela had been such a comfort! She missed her gentle ways. Of course, Mercedes might inherit that, it was still too soon to tell.

Adela had been diagnosed with diabetes when she was just a girl. A careful diet and medication kept her just as vibrant as the others. But when she married and she and Claudio found themselves pregnant, Mamá was afraid for her. The doctor had warned against it, but Adela only laughed. She said, "I will not avoid death if in doing so I must avoid life as well! Claudio is my husband. The rest is up to the Lord."

Mamá smoothed her hair. She knew better than to argue with her oldest daughter. And Adela had positively glowed when Mercedes was born, so rosy and strong; with such a lusty yelp. Everybody laughed when the doctor slapped her bottom; everyone except Adela. Mute with joy, she could only hold out her arms for her precious love.

Months later, Mamá discovered Adela crying over the baby. A chill gripped her. "Adelina! What is wrong?" She put her arms around her daughter. "Are you tired? Do you need more help with the baby? Why don't you ask Modesta – or Trinidad – to come and stay with you for a while?"

"Ha!" Adela had wiped her eyes, smiling at the thought of either one of her sisters getting up at night to change a crying baby, wiping spit-up from her shirt or rocking endlessly in an attempt to lull Mercedes back to sleep.

Mamá laughed too. "Shall I come then, *Querida*?"

Adela kissed her mother and reached for Mercedes again. "It's not that, Mamá. I don't mind the work. And what would Papá and Baby and Carlos do without you?"

Mamá stroked her back. "Then what?" She made a silent prayer that it wasn't the thought of death that made her eldest cry. She was so pale, so thin. She'd lost all her baby weight and more.

"I don't want less work, Mamá," Adela whispered with a catch in her voice. "I want more." Her eyes filled again and in those eyes Mamá saw longing for her unborn children. Adela didn't care to live a long life; she only

wanted more children in the life that she had.
"It's silly, isn't it? I have so much richness
now..."

Mamá hugged her, gently took the baby from
her arms. "Ah, *sí*, all the richness God provides."

But Trini went to stay with Adela and her little
family after all. Later Trini told Mamá how they
laughed and got in each other's way in that tiny
kitchen, the one bathroom. She confessed
minding at first the bland assumption that she
didn't care to watch television. It seemed they
only turned it on when Claudio wanted to see
sports. But after a while, Trini discovered she
preferred evenings spent in long conversations
with her sister, reminiscing about their childhood, listening to her musings about married life
with all its joy and pain, imagining the brilliant
success little Mercedes would achieve one day,
her fairy-tale life.

"Well," Mamá said returning to the kitchen,
"that was good for Trinidad. She got to see true
love in action. Real sacrifice." She lifted the cloth
covering her bread dough, punched it down for
the second time, kneading and stroking until it
resembled a very large, very smooth stone.
Then she rubbed her hands together, balling up
the bits of flour that clung to her fingers,
allowing them to fall back into the bowl. She
worked the dough again and began the task of
dividing it into four equal portions, then she
kneaded each lump in turn.

Yes, Trinidad would one day make a proper
wife. If only she would come home! New York

was so very far away. It loomed as a dangerous place in Mamá's mind. Trini had the boldness of deed and sense of adventure that her father possessed – she was the only one to move away. Mamá smiled. Her third daughter would do well if she could learn to be patient.

Mamá knit her brow. Modesta had rushed into marriage after Adela wed Claudio. What did she need to learn? Ah, she reminded herself, Modesta was a Méndez, she would figure it out; and more importantly, she was God's child as well.

Answer To Whispered Prayers

"Now what? Mamá, I only married him because it was time!"

"Time, *M'ija?*"

"Yes, time; my time. Time to have a husband,
children, my own family. You know my heart's
always belonged to Clau..."

"Modesta, hush! Your sister gone to her
Savior less than a year ago, and here you are,
coveting what was hers?"

"I know, I know. I'm a monster." Modesta
covered her face with her hands.

Mamá put her arms around her elegant
daughter, stroked her perfect hair. "There, there.
You are no monster. It's just the doctor's verdict
that's upset you. Remember, he is not God.
Anything may still happen."

"Mamá, it wasn't a verdict! It can't be
changed! It was the result of a test. Many tests.
And they all said the same thing. I will never
have children. I cannot!" If Modesta allowed
herself the luxury of tears, she would have
dissolved in a flood of mourning for things
she could not have. But such indulgence was
weakness to her. She stiffened. "Mamá," she

said hoarsely, "do you think God's punishing me?"

"Oh, *Querida!* Punishing you for what?"

Modesta's face hardened. "You know," she whispered.

Mamá sighed and patted her daughter's back. "Love is not a crime; wanting children is no sin. And your sister would have been the first to understand. You wouldn't guess it, but she had a trouble like this too."

Modesta blanched. "Adela? How could she? She had Mercedes!"

"You don't think she intended Mercedes to be an only child, do you?"

Modesta frowned.

"Oh, *hijita*, how can I make you understand? To those without children, even one seems such richness! But, a mother doesn't want the second child any less than the first. In fact, she wants the second even more."

Modesta stared. "You mean...? But she seemed so happy! She never said anything to..."

"No."

"So I just assumed she and Claudio were satisfied the way they were. I mean, he doesn't make that much money and they have that little house and she doesn't work – didn't work. I didn't see how they could afford to...she wanted more? She tried?"

"Since the day Mercedes was born, as soon as she was able, Adela began to try again." Mamá stepped into the kitchen, lit the flame under what was left of the morning coffee. She leaned toward the open window over the sink.

A small breeze wafted the scent of Indian summer into the house. "I only know this because I found her crying one day." She turned back to Modesta. "She was in her kitchen, holding little Mercedes. Remember how she used to keep the cradle next to her, in the room wherever she was working? She couldn't be away from that child for ten minutes!" Mamá shook her head and clucked. "There she was, holding the baby, rocking her back and forth in her arms, trying to sing and choking on tears. Her period had come. Again."

"Huh." Modesta chewed her lip. "Her little life always seemed so perfect to me."

"Perhaps your little life seems perfect, too."

"Mine?" Modesta sank onto one of the dining room chairs, offended that the description "little life" should be applied to hers. She tried to push aside a pile of books, to make room for her purse on the table. The effort was too great. She hung the purse on the back of her chair instead.

Her mother poured coffee into thin china cups. Modesta drank hers black, but Mamá stirred milk into her own, studying the cup's chipped rim, its handle that had been glued on so many times it wasn't straight anymore. She would not throw it out. It was from the first set of china she and Papá bought. And besides, there was still some good use left in it.

"Mamá," Modesta leaned forward, "how did she get over it?"

"Adela? I'm not sure she did. There wasn't much time, after all, and it can take years to understand, even longer to accept." She handed

Modesta her cup and sat down across from her.
"At least it did for me."

"For you? You mean...? Understand what?"

"That some things simply must be left to God.
He really does know best." Mamá smiled into her
cup, waiting for Modesta to roll her eyes, click
her tongue. But she didn't.

Instead she sat up straighter, eyes wide.
"Mamá, that's what Adela used to say! That was
her answer to everything."

"Yes, yes, she had the faith, but she was not
given the opportunity to endure." Mamá reached
across the table and took Modesta's hand. "You
try and you fail and you try again. If you fail
again, is it really failure, or is it just that your
family is complete? As God wishes it to be?" She
paused. "Modesta, when you were little, do you
remember the day you stopped playing?"

"When I stopped playing?"

"You and Adela and Trini, well, Trini was a
baby, but you and Adela used to play dolls for
hours – for days! Do you remember?"

Modesta smiled. It was so soothing, the bitter
coffee, Mamá's cluttered house, her patience.
"Of course! We used to take those dolls, our
baby dolls, everywhere. Adela played with hers
till she was thirteen."

"And you stopped when you were eleven. Do
you remember?"

Modesta nodded. "I came to you and I said I
don't know what to do. I didn't want to play and
I didn't know what else there was."

"Do you remember how you felt?"

Modesta frowned at her cup. "Yes. I was at a complete loss."

"And I told you to read a book, go for a walk, work on that embroidery you had started..."

"The pillow cases! But I didn't want to do those things because they weren't as much fun as playing. Or as playing used to be."

"It took you a week or two, but soon you were planning a sleepover, learning to make *empanadas*. You started listening to music. You noticed boys. You left playing in the past. And your sister eventually followed. And years later, Trini. We go through changes. It happens to everyone."

"But Mamá..."

"*Querida*, when God takes something away, He provides something else in its place. You must trust more. We are on God's path, not one created from our own desires."

Modesta smiled to herself. *How like Mamá!* She relaxed her shoulders, leaned back in her chair. She could feel the strap of her new purse push against her shoulder blade. She loved that purse. Paul had smiled indulgently when she brought it home. He'd said, "Do you need a new wardrobe to go with this bag or will the old one do?"

"Mamá, did you tell all this to Adela?"

Her mother nodded. "I don't know whether she truly understood. As I say, it took me years, and she was so young." The *when she died* hung in the air between them, though neither spoke the words. The women finished their coffee.

Modesta carried her mother's cup to the sink and stood for a moment, looking out the window. The bird feeder was full again. Mamá kept it so. She fed the birds, the animals, the family, from time to time a neighbor, never asking anything for herself, content with her life, her family – unless...? "Mamá!" Modesta spun around. "Is that how you had María Elena? She wasn't an accident after all?"

Her mother smiled. "Modesta, there are no accidents. There are prayers and there are answers. It is what makes each life perfect."

Unbidden and Authentic

Trini could toss a tortilla from lid to basket and drop a new circle of dough in its place in three seconds flat. She knew this because she counted every time. And even though she might never rival her mother, who could erect towers of fluffy tortillas without minding the hot stove or the burned fingertips, she was pleased with her efforts. She would surprise Carlos – two surprises really, fresh tortillas and her news: she was thinking of moving back home.

"Mamá!" Trini ducked into the utility room. Her mother was washing, lifting the soaking garments into the wringer; guiding them through another tub of water to rinse. "Mamá, I'm doing the last one."

Her mother sniffed the air. "Burning the last one?"

"Oh shit! Oops, sorry!" Trini flew back to the stove. "Shoot shoot shoot shoot shoot," she muttered, gingerly depositing the last tortilla into the garbage and fanning the air with a dishtowel.

"Hey! Look who's home!" The door banged shut behind Carlos. He grinned at his sister.

"You're making tortillas? Wait a minute – what have you done with our mother?"

Trini laughed. "Surprise. I made a whole batch, see?"

Carlos dropped his load of books on an already cluttered table and lifted a corner of the basket's cloth covering. "Oh, wow. Boy, oh boy!" He removed a tortilla from the exact center of the pile, juggled it briefly and jammed the whole thing in his mouth.

"Hey, slow down. Save some for the rest of us!"

"Is everyone coming?" Carlos mumbled with his mouth full. When Trini nodded he made a face.

She crossed her brown arms. "What's that supposed to mean? You love having the family around."

"First of all, you know what it means." He swallowed hard and reached for another. "And second of all, all of them?"

Trini nodded again.

"They're gonna scare BOB." Carlos folded this tortilla and carefully tore it in two. He gave half to his sister.

"Who?"

"Remember I told you about my weird friend – well, accomplice really, he'd never admit to anything so banal as friendship. He's coming over so I can show him my new script. Only he doesn't know it, which is why I invited him here in the first place because like I said, he's so weird. Plus he's shy. Anyway, I might want him to be in the film. If we make it. I think."

"Oh yeah. Bob."

Carlos shook his head. "You still don't get it." He swallowed the last of his tortilla and wiped his fingers on his jeans.

"What? I only said his name."

"No, you didn't, but never mind." Carlos was already rifling through the books and papers he'd dumped on the table.

"Hey, these are good." Trini sounded surprised. "The new script in there?"

"Somewhere," he muttered. They heard a truck pull into the dirt driveway.

Trini looked out the window. "What's Nunzio driving now?"

Carlos grinned. "After considerable study and exhaustive research, he selected the most dependable American-made truck he could find, with the best EPA and safety rating. Ta-da-a-a!" Carlos made a flourishing motion with his arm.

"Oh, yeah... I think Mamá told me the red part. But all his trucks are red, aren't they?" She chuckled and then gave her younger brother a shove. "Don't just stand there – go help him."

"Are you kidding? Me help him?" Carlos shook his head and slammed out the kitchen door.

Trini watched him lope up the hill to Nunzio's shiny red Ford. Nunzio swung his legs out of the truck cab and the rest of him slowly followed. Her big brother never did anything quickly. He dropped a watermelon into Carlos' arms, nearly sending him reeling down the hill again. Carlos laughed and tried to gesture with his arms stretched around the melon until Nunzio relieved him of it.

Trini loved to see her brothers together, one so vast and stoic, the other like a firecracker, ready to explode. She went to fetch her mother. "Mamá! Leave the wash. I'll finish. Nunzio is here. Where's Dad?"

"This is the last load, Trinidad. You can help me hang it."

"Mamá, why don't we just use the dryer?"

"The sheets will not smell as sweet dried that way."

"But the picnic? Just this once..."

Mamá heaved a plastic basket of wet laundry to the top of the dryer. "Very well." She smoothed her hair, a familiar gesture when she was making a concession. "Your father?" She began loading laundry into the dryer. "He must still be in the woods. Can you hear the chainsaw?"

Trini shook her head. "I don't think so."

Trini and her mother went outside to take down the clothes line, stretched halfway up the hill, from the buckeye to the sagging staircase on the side of the garage and across again to a post which stood at the corner of the deck. The garage was dug into the hillside, so that the top part was level with the driveway, and underneath was a musty, dark storage room for tools, cans of fuel, the heavy duty mower that had never known a seat. Papa would no sooner sit to cut the grass than he would sit to cut down a tree with his chain saw. The storage room had that great smell of metal and gasoline. When she was little, Trini wanted to be a gas station attendant because of that smell. Of course, gas station attendants didn't pump gas anymore. Trini wondered, did anyone else still hang wash?

"Hey, Ma!" Nunzio held the melon in one arm and lifted his mother in an embrace with the other.

Mamá took the melon and when all three of her children protested said, "Now, now, I've carried more than this before. Go find your father."

Nunzio turned toward the woods. "Chicken, Mamá?"

"*Arroz con pollo*. Your favorite. And Trini made tortillas."

"Funny," Nunzio grinned over his shoulder. "I didn't smell anything burning!"

Trini threw a clothespin at him and then had to go pick it up. "Carlos," she said, "help me wind up the clothesline. Mamá, we'll do it; you go relax."

Mamá smilcd. She shielded her eyes with her free hand. "I see Mr. Kramer's car in his driveway. Your little sister must be back from 4-H."

"That's why it's so quiet!" Carlos murmured.

"Not for long," Trini said. "I wondered where Baby was."

Mamá shook her head as she descended to the kitchen. "No, no. Don't call her that. She's changed her name again." She disappeared into the house.

Carlos and Trini looked at each other. "Again?"

María Elena, or Baby, as they liked to refer to their baby sister, was born seven years after

Carlos, the supposed last child. When she was six and Carlos old enough to be steeped in the Catholic rite of Confirmation, Baby asked him what that meant.

"It means if you really want to be a Catholic, you promise to follow all the rules and then you get to pick your favorite saint and take his name."

"Oh. Like a reward?"

"Um, more like a reminder. Who's your favorite saint?"

Without hesitation she replied, "Mary Magdalene."

He whistled. "Boy, oh boy."

Suddenly, Baby brightened. "You may call me that from now on."

"Magdalena?" he asked hopefully.

She gave her head a very determined shake. Baby was Mary Magdalene for the next seven months – both names, in English, every time or she wouldn't even acknowledge the speaker.

From where they stood, Carlos and Trini could see their little sister go into the Kramers' house, probably for a snack.

"So, what's this one about?" Trini said. "The script I mean."

"Oh, it's a sci-fi thing about a guy who leaves home in search of a legendary comet."

"Why's he looking for a comet?"

"Well, he's a loner, but the kind of guy who drags his solitude around like a weight. He lives in the woods, hunts for his food and all that and then one day he starts to notice how the animals all have families: birds, squirrels, deer, what have you, and he starts to feel like something's missing in his life. So, he's tromping around, sleeping on the ground, cooking over campfires, and one night he has this dream. He dreams up a creature, more beautiful than anything he's ever seen, stronger, sweeter, and he recognizes this as the missing part of his life or maybe himself. The next night he dreams it again, and the next and in his dreams he begins tracking the creature, wanting to possess it. So when he finally gets a good look at it, it turns out to be a girl."

"Naturally."

"No, not that. Remember, this is all a dream. Anyway, our hunter considers how best to capture his prey and he decides to build a trap for it. So he actually starts building a trap. In his waking life, I mean. We'll make this part really elaborate in the film. So, he builds the trap, gets exhausted, falls asleep right by it and naturally, the creature appears in his dreams, watching him. So, first he baits the trap with food, which snares a fox and the second time he baits it with silk and gems, you know, stuff girls like – and he lures a crow. He catches the fox and the crow in his dream, but each time he wakes up, the bait is gone in the real trap. The third time it works."

"What's the bait?"

"He is."

"What?"

"Yeah, he thinks about what draws people together and he realizes it's not wealth, but tragedy. If someone's hurt what do you do?"

"Run over to make sure he's okay."

"See? So he pretends to be hurt, actually he cuts his leg so he isn't pretending entirely. She appears in real life now. She creeps over to him, sees he's hurt, unarmed, as vulnerable as she is. So, gently, carefully, she heals him with a touch. They talk and she confesses that she was both the fox and the crow. She tells him she's always around him in some form or another. He asks her name and she says she doesn't have one; she has no need for a name. She says, 'Would you name the air you breathe? The wind that caresses you? The heavens above?' Then he notices she has a kind of sunflower shape right about here," Carlos touched Trini's neck. "He asks her what it is and she tells him it's the mark of the comet."

"The mark of the comet..."

"Yeah. So he's all curious about how she got it and what it means. He asks her and she says, 'You must return.' He says something like, 'Return where? Here?' He presses her, but she won't say anything else.

So then, the next night, he dreams of the comet. It's beautiful and wild and – we'll have to use special effects to bring that off."

"Huh."

"During the day he gets worried because the girl didn't show up and he thinks, what if she never shows up again?"

"So she really does exist somewhere? His dreams are real?"

Carlos nodded. "He keeps dreaming of the comet and in a panic, he decides that it must hold the answer to her whereabouts, so he starts tracking the comet."

"But how do you catch a comet?"

"Yeah, right. How can you catch it; how can you lure it? So now he's obsessed with this chase. He's searching for it all the time, asleep, awake. One day when he's completely discouraged, just about ready to give up, he catches a glimpse of the comet's tail, trailing around one of his suns!"

"Okay, wait..."

"Yeah, see, even though he only sees one sun at any given time, he's convinced that there really are two."

"Like twins?"

"Kind of. That's how he thinks the other side of the world lives. It makes sense to him. It'll be like, I don't know, an accepted belief or part of the girl's story or something."

"But he never really sees it?"

"No. The hunter separates seeing and believing as two totally separate activities. Abilities. He's got the courage to believe without seeing."

"So this guy's pursuing something he can't really see, based on his belief that it exists, in order to find something that really exists, based on what he's seen in his dreams?"

"Yeah, that's it. He'll have occasional sightings of the comet, but that's mostly for the audience's sake. So anyway, in his quest, the hunter discovers a sacred scroll that reveals another definition of the word comet: a beautiful longhaired being. He learns that the ancients

considered comets living things. Creatures, indi-
viduals. So the girl could actually be the spirit of
the comet and his only way of finding her is to
find and capture the comet.

"So then he thinks, if a comet is a living thing,"
here Carlos slowed down, ran his fingers through
his hair, "maybe everything has a beautiful soul.
This gets him more excited and it feeds his
obsession. Pretty soon all creation comes alive
to him and he sees things he never did before.
So he starts asking everyone, every thing for
help: animals, rocks, wind, clouds. And they all
point to the trail of the comet. Eventually, his
memory of the girl and his vision of the comet
become one and he convinces himself he's
actually in love with the comet."

"In love? Stalking, as it were?"

Carlos smiled, nodded. "We'll have to find a
way to compress the hunt and still show how
he's totally consumed by it."

"Hey you guys! You're here!" Baby came
galloping up the driveway. She was taller than
when Trini had seen her last, thinner, her hair
longer.

"Baby!" Trini held out her arms.

She stopped in mid flight. "That's not my
name."

"Oh, come here! Who cares? Want me to call
you Madam President?" Trini ran up and forced a
hug upon her little sister.

"Don't be ridiculous. Women aren't presi-
dents – ow! Don't squeeze me so hard – yet!"

"*Señorita*," Carlos regarded his sister earnestly, "by which of your glorious titles are we addressing you today?"

"Not just today. I'm through with Baby and with María Elena. Forever."

"Don't forget Mary Magdalene."

"Please! I was just a child back then. You may call me," raising her chin, tilting her head for dramatic effect, "ME."

"Me?" Trini blinked. "Won't that be kind of – confusing?" What she meant was conceited, but she didn't like to pick a fight.

Baby sighed.

"Wait a minute," Carlos said, his jaw dropping. "Holy – you mean M-E, don't you?" He spelled it this time.

Relief poured over Baby's face. "Yes! Of course."

"Initials?" Trini asked.

Baby answered patiently, "No. You don't spell it out every time, it's..."

Carlos interrupted. He nodded as he repeated, "*ME*. Just like – *boy, oh boy!*"

Trini threw her hands in the air and headed back to the house. "It's like we don't even speak the same language!"

The kitchen was warm, filled with the smell of chicken and sweet onions. Mamá was browning the rice. "Nunzio find your father yet?"

Trini shook her head. "ME is here."

"What kind of talk is that, baby talk?"

"Yes. But don't call her that."

Mamá frowned.

Trini lingered, touching things, lifting lids. She wondered if she should say something to Mamá about moving back, but decided, no. Why get her hopes up until she was absolutely sure?

Two more cars drove up. First, a navy blue station wagon holding Claudio and his little daughter, Mercedes. It was still a shock to see them without Adela. And just behind them, a black BMW crunched over the stones and little clumps of dirt, carrying the beautifully perfect Modesta and Paul.

Paul and Claudio greeted one another in the driveway while Modesta led Mercedes down the hill. Trini and her mother watched the pair lift their arms and run.

"They're going to take a tumble," Mamá said softly. "But just look at that child's face!" Mercedes glowed with pleasure. Everyone had been so worried about her when her mother died. She and Claudio seemed fine now.

Modesta knelt to tie Mercedes' shoe. Trini watched her watching Claudio.

"Aunt Modesta," Mercedes broke the spell. "You don't have to..."

"Sh. It's all right," she smiled up at Mercedes. "I don't mind."

Mercedes watched her aunt with surprise. She couldn't get used to her beautiful aunt waiting on her, fawning over her like she was a baby. She shrugged. It was probably just because she didn't have any children of her own. Poor Auntie Mo – Aunt Modesta. She kept forgetting she wasn't supposed to call her that anymore.

Modesta grinned up at the child. "One more time?"

Mercedes nodded.

Together they pranced to the top of the hill again, Mercedes jumping and skipping around her graceful aunt. This time Claudio couldn't help but notice them, hair flying, perfume on the wind. He smiled.

"Modesta!" Trini wrapped her arms around her sister's designer shirt, felt her heart pumping wildly, her body warm from running. "Nice running outfit!"

"I liked it this morning, but now I wish I was dressed like Mercedes!" Both girls watched Mamá hugging the little girl like she'd never let her go.

"My turn, my turn!" Trini grabbed Mercedes, tickling her and planting big kisses on her head.

"Aunt Trini! You always do that!" Mercedes giggled.

"Baby!" Modesta called. "Mercedes, go find Aunt Baby to play with!"

"No, no," Trini interrupted. "She doesn't go by that anymore."

Modesta sighed. "What is it now?"

"Just call her me."

"You?"

"Call Aunt Baby *Aunt Trini* too?" Mercedes asked doubtfully.

"No, no. Me. *Me.*"

"Aunt Mimi?" Modesta frowned. "Mercedes, call your Aunt Baby, Aunt Mimi from now on. And don't ask!"

Trini started to correct them, then changed her mind. It didn't really matter. Mercedes would be forgiven and Modesta was going to slip up anyway. She shrugged and went to look for Carlos.

He was behind the barn, watching Nunzio split wood for a fire. Claudio and Dad were drinking beer. Trini kissed her father on the cheek, inhaled his scent of cut grass and new wood. She gave Claudio a warm greeting. He smiled at her, asked if Mamá needed help.

"Of course not – you know Mamá. Dad, were you clearing the woods again?"

"I made a whole new path! Didn't you hear the chainsaw? You and Carlos go take a look. Baby and Mercedes will love it!"

"Good idea. C'mon Carlitos."

They marched up the hill, around a patch of poison ivy and into the crunchy cool forest. Then, almost immediately they stepped into sunlight again. Their father had cut a swath through the brush, at least six feet wide, circling trees and rounding hills.

"Man, look at this!" Trini said under her breath.

"Yeah, I know. He's nuts!"

"Carlos! Don't talk about Dad that way!"

"Easy for you to say," he muttered. "You don't have to follow in his footsteps."

"Sure I do. We all do. Except maybe for Baby."

Carlos smiled at the ground and nodded. They walked in silence for a while.

Trini picked up a leaf. "This is red already!" She turned it in her hand. "You wanna finish telling me?"

"What?"

"The Comet! What happens next?"

"Oh, yeah. Where were we? Oh – okay. So, chasing his dream, the hunter is drawn back to his own home."

Trini blushed, but Carlos didn't notice. Had he guessed her plan? "You mean back to his actual house?"

"Well, not exactly. First, it's just his galaxy, his solar system, but he's so obsessed with the chase, he doesn't even notice. Not until he's orbiting his home planet."

"Which is?"

Carlos smiled. "Earth."

They heard voices calling. "Hey, you guys! Wait up!" It was Modesta, flanked by Baby and Mercedes.

"Hello, ME." Carlos was frankly delighted with her new name.

Baby smiled. Her Carlitos *would* be the first one to get it!

Some ended up calling her Mia. Some Mimi. Her mother stubbornly stuck to María Elena and her father now called her "Baby-oops!" Often Claudio or Nunzio or one of her sisters would forget and call her Baby, but Baby only thought of herself as ME, so convinced was she of its absolute perfection. It was short. It was sweet. It was bold. It reminded her gently of the name she had been given, while allowing her the freedom to define herself. She occasionally wondered why nobody else had chosen it.

By the time BOB arrived, everyone was sitting on the patio or in the grass around the house, balancing paper plates weighted with mounds of chicken and rice, scooping their food with tortillas. Carlos wiped his hands on his jeans and went up to the driveway to welcome his friend, to prepare him for the challenge that was his family.

"So." BOB jerked his chin toward the group below. "Family unit, huh?"

Carlos nodded. "That's my family. They prefer not to be referred to as a unit though."

"Who's who?"

"My brother Nunzio with my Dad, Claudio next to him. He used to be married to my sister Adela. That's his daughter, little Mercedes."

"Cool name."

"And next to her is Modesta."

BOB squinted and pressed his lips together.

"And her husband, Paul, and my sister, Trini – Trinidad."

"And your mom, obviously. Who's the squirt?"

"That's María Elena. You better let her tell you her name herself."

"Cool, man. Like a pride."

"Oh, you got that right. Way too much pride! But listen, before we go down, I want to tell you about a script I'm working on..."

"Mercedes, is that your fourth tortilla?" Claudio looked stern.

"But Daddy, it's the best part!"

Trini beamed at her. "Smart kid. Takes after her aunt, obviously."

Claudio shook his head, frowned and mouthed, "No more," to his daughter while listening to Nunzio tell stories about work. At times like this he missed his wife. Adela would have watched over Mercedes, would have made sure she ate right. He was, no doubt, spoiling the child.

Modesta moved closer to Mercedes. "Here, Honey. Here's what you do. Wrap some chicken inside, see? It's like a little tiny mouthful in a blanket! And no fork! *Voilá!*"

Mercedes giggled. "I'm not a baby, Aunt Modesta." But she obediently ate what her aunt gave her.

Claudio shot Modesta a grateful look. "So, Paul," he turned to her husband, "how's the fleet?"

"The cars? Jag's in the shop again. The Beamer's great, but it's worse than the Mustang in any weather, and I am not taking my baby out of storage this winter. What we really need is a truck."

Modesta sighed and made a face.

Paul gestured toward her. "See what I mean? Plus, then we'd have to rent another garage or something."

Trini winced. No one seemed to notice how obnoxious they were. Perhaps the others didn't care that Paul and Modesta were rich and they were not. What would it be like, she wondered, to immerse herself in all this again?

"Trinidad," Mamá motioned to Carlos and BOB, still standing on the hill by the cars. "Tell those two to come down and eat! It's a sin; two skinny boys and all this food!"

"Sure, Mamá." Trini pushed back her bangs and climbed to where the boys were leaning against BOB's Volkswagen. "Hey, guys," she said. "Mamá says come down and eat." Carlos was watching BOB's face. They didn't answer.

"Sounds interesting," BOB was saying, "but what do you want me to do? I'm not an actor or anything. I mean, I could take a look at the writing if you want." He glanced at Trini, then immediately looked away again.

"It's more about attitude than acting," Carlos said.

Trini thought, so this is weird BOB. Being closer to him did nothing for his looks: medium height, painfully thin, pale, hooknose and thick black hair. He looked like one of those pictures of people from the Depression, or maybe from the Holocaust. She smiled, but he would not return her look.

"Hey, Trini," Carlos said. "This is BOB."

With head ducked, BOB stuck out a clammy hand for her to shake.

"Pleased to meet you!" she chirped. "Carlos tells me you're quite talented."

"Ha!" He suddenly became very interested in the gravel at his feet.

Trini grinned at Carlos. "You better come down so Mamá can feed you."

Surprise emboldened BOB. He suddenly faced her. "Do I look hungry?" He seemed taller now, somehow challenging. Trini felt her face flush.

"No," she said slowly, caught in his gaze. "You look like you're starving." Then she turned and ran back down the hill.

When Trini reached the patio, it sounded like Paul and Modesta were ganging up on Claudio.

"You have to put aside just this much each month," Paul was saying, writing on a paper napkin. "Then, when Mercedes is seventeen... for sake of argument, let's say eighteen..."

"Oh, leave him alone! Here, Claudio, try my ambrosia. You loved it last time!" Modesta put a spoonful of the sweet goo into his protesting mouth.

Paul leaned closer. "Modesta, you've made a career out of telling people what to do! Talk to your brother-in-law. A little free advice won't hurt. Tell her, Claudio!"

Claudio pointed at his full mouth and shook his head. He and Modesta were laughing, trying not to laugh. They looked at each other with camaraderie, a shared twinkling of the eye. Trini stiffened. Paul just kept scribbling on the napkin.

"Where's ME?" Carlos stood with his hands on his hips, looking over the family group. He had introduced BOB to everyone else.

"That supposed to be existential?" Claudio asked.

"You mean rhetorical." Modesta said.

"No, no! I mean, I mean, what the hell – excuse me, Mamá – I mean, what's that supposed to mean? You're standing right here!" Claudio laughed.

"Aunt Mimi?" Mercedes piped up.

"Who?" Carlos asked.

"She means María Elena," Trini said.

"What are you all going on about?" Mamá interrupted, passing the tortilla basket around again. "María Elena ran off as soon as she saw you two coming down the hill."

BOB looked at Carlos. "Forget it, man. I'm never gonna remember their names anyway."

Carlos nodded, and handed BOB a chicken leg. "It's a lot."

For a skinny guy, BOB ate non-stop. Mamá was flattered, Trini amused, and Modesta frustrated that she got no reaction whatsoever from the newcomer. Trini wondered if he ate from hunger or from fear. She sidled up to her brother.

"So how does it end?"

He drank from a can of grape soda. "Comet chase?"

"Of course. What else?"

"What's she up to?" BOB asked, filling his plate for the third time.

"Home stretch," Carlos smiled.

"Did you tell him the whole thing already?" Trini pointed at BOB with her chin.

Carlos nodded. "So the traveler ends up following the tail of the comet back to his own planet..."

BOB smiled at his chicken. "I love the two suns."

"And when he reaches Earth, after chasing this comet for like, forever, his hair is long and his clothes are all unkempt and the trail leads him to this big hole in the ground that he thinks must have been made by the comet." Carlos took a drink of his soda. He wiped his mouth with the back of his hand. "And it's all full of water."

"Like rain?"

"Yeah, maybe. It's like a pond. So he leans over to take a drink, and the tips of his hair fall into the water."

BOB spread his hands in the air. "And it makes the water ripple so that it looks like there are two suns behind him, on either side of his reflection with his long hair dangling in the water."

The boys smiled at each other.

"So? That's it?" Trini squinted up at the sun. "You mean...?"

"A visual metaphor." Carlos crossed his arms over his chest. "Chasing love. Chasing life. Coming home. We'll mix scenes from his en-counter with the girl and the comet chase in with the ripples until the girl and the comet morph into the two suns and they'll converge and light up the man's heart. The light completes the man."

"The light completes the man!" Trini smiled. "And the girl?"

"The female part of himself, the anchor that balances the comet – the inspiration and the adventure."

BOB nodded. "Together they form the 'aha' when you realize that what you've been searching for was in your back pocket all along."

Trini turned toward him. "And you're gonna be in it?"

He looked down. "I am in it." His seriousness made Trini smile.

"You want cake." It was a statement, rather than a question. ME stood with knife poised, ready to slice into the fluffy chocolate frosting that held the yellow layers together. Modesta had brought it. Bought it. The only thing she could bake was *empanadas*, and she wasn't inclined to do this for just any occasion.

BOB nodded, oddly at ease with the youngest Méndez. "Of course. The layer cake is the best example of architecture in the modern world."

"I wish I knew the Pillsbury dough guy," ME said.

"When I was little, I wanted to marry Betty Crocker," BOB replied.

ME hacked a huge chunk and tried to balance it on BOB's limp paper plate.

"Hold still, Bobby."

"It's not Bobby, it's BOB."

"Same thing." She successfully landed the cake in the remnants of his *arroz con pollo*, now just *arroz*.

"No, you mean like Robert Wagner and Robby Douglas and Bob Hope."

"You forgot Bobby Kennedy," ME added.

He looked right in her face. "I'm B-O-B." This time he spelled it to her slowly, loudly, like she was a foreigner or deaf.

"Oh. You mean like ME."

"No. We're all ourselves. You're you, I'm me, only I call myself BOB."

"No, I'm not me. I'm M-E." She spelled it back to him.

He frowned. "M-E? ME?"

"That's it."

"For?"

She looked from side to side.

He whispered. "Is it classified?"

She nodded. "Should be. María Elena."

He blinked. "But that suits you!"

"No, ME."

BOB laughed and laughed.

"Keep still! And what's yours stand for?"

He leaned closer and whispered, "Boy. Oh. Boy."

She brought her small square hand to her mouth to hide the O. "Like ME!"

"Exactly." He smiled.

Trinidad was at the kitchen sink washing up, picking plastic silverware from soggy plates, shoving the remains into a bag that could be knotted and disposed of later. Modesta wandered in with two beers. "Here," she said, handing one to her sister. "You don't want to let me get ahead of you."

Trini took the beer from her jeweled fingers. "Don't worry," she answered. "You won't."

Modesta glanced out the window. "Nunzio's looking good," she ventured. "Now, why doesn't he find a nice girl and settle down?" Her gaze drifted past him to her brother-in-law.

"And Claudio?" Trini refused to tiptoe around her sister.

Modesta's silence filled the little kitchen.

"Don't do it, Mo."

Modesta cringed at the sound of her childhood nickname.

"It makes no sense."

"What do you know of sense?" Modesta threw her head back, gulped the metallic beer. She touched the corners of her shiny red mouth. "Did it make sense for him to fall in love with Adela? And for her to fall for him? She was my safety net. The holy one. The nun. And then to lose her so quickly! Did it make sense that I...I couldn't wait...how could I know..."

"Mo!" Trini grabbed her sister's arms with soapy hands. "He married our sister and you married Paul."

"And does that have to be the end of it?"

"That is the end of it."

Modesta's eyes filled with tears. "I know, I know." She sank onto a chipped wooden chair, shoved against the wall beneath a statue of the Infant of Prague. Jesus gazed down sadly. "And you know what's funny? Now that he's free, he loves his Adelina more than ever."

Trinidad and Modesta both watched Claudio deep in conversation with Nunzio and their father. He was a small, but powerful man, quiet and wistful; with eyes that could melt the heart of any woman. Having to raise a child made him even more attractive to the two sisters, who had none. But Trini had a rule about such things and Modesta had decided years ago that she wanted more.

"And besides," Modesta continued. "I could never..."

"Leave Paul?"

"...make him happy."

Trini studied Claudio, wondering what made him happy. Certainly Modesta did when they first met – before the fighting, before Mo joined an accounting firm, lost weight, bought a wardrobe and a car. And then he had gotten to know Adela. She had made him happy – simple, sweet, religious Adelina, who wanted nothing more than to be a wife and mother. "Mo," Trini whispered suddenly. "Why don't you and Paul have children?"

Modesta bit her lip. She didn't bother with her usual *who has the time* response.

"Oh, dear. I'm so sorry." Trini reached out to touch her sister, but Modesta quickly drew back.

She forced a laugh. "Guess the joke's on me. Aren't you glad you moved away?"

Trini wandered out into the yard. She smiled at her mother, telling a story to Mercedes and the newly christened ME. She passed her father and Nunzio, pretending to discuss sports with Claudio, while secretly tallying up the next day's workload. She circled around the old garage and sank down against the cement block wall, letting the sun warm her face and arms, soaking it all in – home, happiness, family, frustration. She closed her eyes. When she opened them again, there were Carlos and BOB, on either side of her looking down. She took the clip from her hair. Tumbles of brown curls fell around her neck and shoulders.

"So, how long are you staying this time?" Carlos demanded.

"Till tomorrow. Then I'm going home to pack. I'm moving back, Carlitos. It's time to come home." She lifted one hand to shade her eyes. "BOB, will this be your first role?"

BOB stared at her. "As what? Are you offering me a part?"

"No, no! I mean Carlos' comet thing."

"I don't act." He looked disgusted for a moment, but then the corners of his mouth turned up and the unexpected radiance of his smile made Trini blink. "And for your information, the comet thing? It's called: *Glorious Pursuit.*"

Comfort of the Outcast

Why would anyone put a barn here? Right in the middle of a forest? No water, no access... doesn't make sense.

But maybe it wasn't always like that. Maybe in the olden days, back when it was built, maybe someone had cleared the land for a farm and a road. The house must have stood somewhere around here too. If you cock your head to one side and squint, you can almost see a farmer shepherding cows, goats, maybe a horse, into the barn's cozy recesses filled with sweet dusty hay. If you close your eyes you can smell it, especially on a hot summer's day.

Hear that dog barking, in the distance?

Shut your eyes tight, and think. A dog could've barked when a cow strayed or a fox approached. He might've barked to welcome his master. Or his mistress. Maybe the farmer was married. They say Abe Lincoln (or was it George Washington?) passed through here once. Maybe the farmer met him. One day, he put on his good suit and he took his wife, gathered his brood, all spit and polish, to meet the President. And the President could have come back for a piece of pie and said, "First-rate farm, you have here! Fine livestock, fine barn!"

Only, that would have been long before this barn was built.

But that farmer, he could have had a wife, children; a pretty daughter, just like the wife. And sons...

Oh, damn it all, maybe he had tall handsome sons who were just pig-headed enough to follow everyone else to war. The Civil War? One of the World Wars? One like this?

They say those wars were different, but the barn wouldn't have known. It stood through weather, through lifetimes of animals, of people. Living things, they come and go. A barn just stands still, slowly crumbling, dissolving back into that from which it came.

And some day, years from now, someone else will pass this way; maybe notice a beam, a piece of foundation rock still holding its own in the sorrowing decay. And if I carve a mark, a cross, some initials on something right here, maybe he'll pause and wonder about the folks who passed by here before him, and whether they had sons.

"What's that you're reading, Dad?" María Elena walked into the living room to find her father standing by a window, an old English textbook in his hands. He wasn't looking at the book though. He had a piece of paper with handwriting on it, tilted toward the waning light.

"It's something your sister wrote, years ago, in school."

"Can I see it?" She read with a frown on her face. "What war?"

"Vietnam."

"Was it, like, an assignment or something?"

"No. She was in eleventh grade when the Jones boys were both killed in battle. She and your mother took some food to the family. Mrs. Jones was nearly insane with grief, wouldn't eat or sleep, wasn't making any sense. It was three deaths, in a way. So when she got back, your sister walked up to the old barn. Came back all red-eyed and wrote this for the school newspaper. She said the thing they don't tell you about war is that the biggest sacrifice isn't the boys who go heaven, but the anguish of those left behind."

"Did they print it?"

"No." He smiled. "But she didn't care. She said the writing was enough."

"Which one wouldn't care? Trini or Modesta?"

"Oh," he passed his hand over his eyes. "Your sister Adela. Adelina wrote that." He placed the page carefully inside the textbook and slipped it back on the shelf, next to the Bible.

"That sounds like her, Dad. Like what I remember of her."

He touched María Elena's cheek. "She was empathetic to the sufferings of others, but much too young to know. It's not just war, María Elena. All death is like that." Then he put on his old straw hat and went outside to mow the field.

Gracious Love Appear

BOB and Carlos leaned over the railing, squinting at the ground far below. On its icy crust stood a tin can, a tiny gaping mouth among the rocks. "It'll be a miracle if you make it," Carlos observed, his breath coming out in little puffs of steam.

"Then that's what we'll call this one: Miracles." BOB was all seriousness, though a sneering smile stretched across his face.

Carlos nodded. "*Milagros.*"

BOB bent over the bridge railing as far as he could and dropped a small silver object. The boys heard a ping as it bounced off the rocks and disappeared into remnants of snow. "Shit."

Now Carlos straightened up, tucked in his chin and with elbows clenched against his sides, he too leaned forward and brought a piece of silver clear up to his nose, before closing one eye and letting go. Ping. "Shit."

They kept at it all afternoon. When the sun had lowered and the air chilled significantly, hunger drove them from the bridge, into the frozen rubble below to collect their missiles. There, glints of silver shone in and around the snowy rocks, like proverbial seed scattered on unforgiving ground. They were stones, lucky stones painted silver. "Where'd you get all the painted rocks, anyway?" Carlos asked, filling his pockets.

"Made 'em. Painted them, I mean."

Carlos picked up the can.

"Hey, man. Don't do that!"

"Do what?"

"You can't touch the can! We're not done."

"What do you mean?"

"Nobody won yet!"

Carlos shook his head.

The day before, they had spent the afternoon with their slingshots, shooting icicles that hung from the roof of an abandoned warehouse. First, just shooting from where they stood, then backing up, more and more, behind trees, then in the trees, shooting from their branches.

Last weekend their adventuring was walking on exposed pipe in a new development. Barefoot. With their eyes closed. BOB had accused Carlos of cheating. "Hey man," BOB stuck a bony finger in Carlos' face. "You have to figure, what would I do if this was the only way over a huge ravine and I was, I don't know, blind or something!"

"Were I 'blind or something' I don't think I'd be crossing ravines on pipes, without my shoes, particularly in winter."

"But what if you HAD to!"

"Like someone put a gun to my head?"

"Yeah, or stuck a knife in your back, or..."

"Man, you really have it in for the blind, don't you?"

Carlos chuckled now. "Why are you so crazy about playing games?"

"It prepares you. Besides, if you don't play, you can't win." BOB was busy counting his silver stones. "Some of them must have ricocheted off." They kept searching.

"So," BOB cleared his throat. "Your sister's nice. Cute, I mean."

"Modesta? Yeah, everyone says she's hot. But, nice?"

"No, no. The other one."

"María Elena?"

"What do you take me for, man! She's like, ten years old!"

"She's fifteen, and she'll give you a knuckle sandwich to prove it!" Carlos laughed. Suddenly he stopped. "You mean Trini?"

"Yeah. You probably don't see it, because she's your sister."

"Huh. You mean because, like, we took baths together, threw rocks at each other, thought each was the first to tell the other about sex? Well, Mo's my sister too, and I can still see the difference between them."

"You said yourself, Modesta's not nice."

Carlos sat back on his heels. "Yeah. You're right. Trini is a sport." He watched BOB, who seemed to be gathering the silver stones with a certain self-consciousness now. "Why?"

"Why what?"

"Why did you say that?"

"No reason," BOB kept his eyes averted. "Just making conversation."

"Conversation, eh?" Carlos kept searching among the rocks. "So what are we missing?"

"That's it! That's what I'm thinking!" BOB stood up and flung his arms wide. "I mean, sure, we know chicks are only in it for one thing; they just want to suck the power, the life force from us and all that. I mean, it's probably true – it is true – but then you go and you meet one who gets you, no, two, no three, and they're all in the same family – a whole family that gets you, and one especially, is so, well, sexy and amazing and she draws you like a burning magnet and you're using all your strength, every ounce of energy you've got to resist and it takes so much effort, you start to wonder why. Why did we ever decide we had to keep away?"

Carlos sat with his mouth open.

"So then you can't help thinking, what am I missing?" BOB was sweating now. His pockets bulged.

"I was talking about your stupid painted rocks."

"Oh."

Carlos stared at BOB. "So ask her out."

"Oooh, no!"

"Well, if you're so damn certain that resisting her is wrecking your life, what else is there?"

"She's your sister, man."

"Hey, I don't like it any more than you do, but what choice do you have? I mean, if it's gonna drive you nuts – personally I think that ship sailed long ago – but if it's making you even more nuts than you already are...?"

BOB's shoulders relaxed. "So it's okay with you then. If I do it."

Carlos was working on a painted stone wedged tightly between two rocks. The more he scraped and clawed at their icy surfaces, the more his fingers ached. BOB watched silently until the stone was dislodged and Carlos turned it over in his hands, as if it was a precious thing. "I said," BOB repeated, "so it's okay with you then? If I do it?"

The sun was almost down. Carlos faced the can, took one step toward it and drew his arm back, hurling the stone with more force than was absolutely necessary. TWANG. It bounced off.

"That my answer?" BOB gave his grimace of a smile.

"What? Yeah. No. Don't worry about it." Carlos walked over to the can and picked it up. "I'll get over it."

BOB shoved his dirty hands through his hair. "I mean, hey, we're presuming she'll say yes. We don't even know if she'll agree to go out with me, but the possibility does exist, and then once I ask it'll be awful if she doesn't go because there's your whole family and I'm sure they'll all know and then whenever..."

"I said I'll get over it," Carlos muttered, one eye closed as he peered into the can. "Of course, Ken'll have to get over it first."

"Who?"

"Her boyfriend. Holy shit." He pulled another stone from his pocket and laid it carefully over the opening. "Talk about *milagros*!"

"I know, I know it's a long shot but..."

"I'll say! It's way too small."

"What?"

"The can! You could throw rocks at it all day and they'd never go in. The opening's just too small."

BOB smiled thoughtfully. "Yeah," he agreed, "It'll be a miracle."

Occupy The Hollow

Well, she was here. Modesta tapped her polished nails on the steering wheel. There was nothing to be gained by waiting. With a deep breath she unfolded herself from the car, straightened her blouse and reached in to lift the warm plate of *empanadas* from the back seat. He'd always loved her *empanadas*. Was she crazy to be doing this? Perhaps she'd lost her mind.

Modesta was not used to being nervous. Exactly four times on her way over (a distance of only 8.2 miles), men had slammed on their brakes, inched along, in some cases nearly colliding with one another as they gawked at the Spanish beauty in the red Jag. Modesta was used to this; indeed, she almost didn't notice it anymore. She knew she'd notice though, when they stopped looking. She twitched her shoulders sharply and rang the bell.

The moment took hours. She nearly fled back to the car, but suddenly here was Claudio, nodding, smiling as though he'd been expecting her.

"Modesta! Lovely. What is it?"

"*Empanadas!*" she answered gaily. She waved the fragrant dish under his nose.

"Oh, my!" Claudio stepped aside to let her enter. "Come in. Come in."

"Thank you." She brushed against him as she strutted to the kitchen. With a quick glance around, Modesta forced her mind to be still, to refrain from making any judgments. "Claudio, I hope I'm not intruding?" She saw a prescription bottle with Adela's name on the windowsill above the sink, a note in her handwriting by the phone. Modesta shivered.

"No, no. I was just going to get a paper to read with my lunch. Mercedes is at school, of course."

"Oh, that's right! Silly me. We'll just keep some of these wrapped for her. She can have them for supper or maybe take them in her lunch tomorrow? I hate for Mercedes to miss out, she just loves *empanadas*..."

"Mo." He was the only one she didn't mind using that name. It brought back nights of hamburger dinners, bubble baths and guitar serenades – like a secret between them, their bittersweet past. Her eyes filled, but still she busied herself finding plates and forks. Claudio took her by the shoulders, firmly. "Mo. Stop." Rigid in his grip, she turned to face him.

"It's just that...I only..." Modesta cleared her throat.

Suddenly his arms went round her. She was taller than he, but only slightly. She curled into him and squeezed her eyes tight. "Mo," he whispered. "It's all right. It's all right. I know."

And he did. He knew she loved him when he married her sister, Adela. He felt it on the day she announced she'd wedded Paul. He could see it in her eyes when Mercedes was christened. (His wife could have chosen Trini or even María Elena for godmother, but no, she must have Modesta!) And although his capacity had been dulled, he knew her love surrounded him again at Adela's funeral.

"Look around you, Mo," he whispered. She opened her eyes, took in the yellowing linoleum floor, dime store café curtains, the Formica table with its battered vinyl chairs. "You only love your dream of me – not the man I am." She moved as though to protest, but he stopped her with a gentle pressure. Claudio smoothed Modesta's very smooth hair, straightened her very straight collar. He was just beginning to understand what his wife had always claimed, that God knew best. "*Empanadas*? My favorite!"

They sat. Modesta watched Claudio devour his lunch. The smooth muscles of his jaw tensed, relaxed, tensed again. Hypnotized, she murmured, "Tell me something, Claudio, why are *empanadas* your favorite?"

"Oh, the surprise I guess." He took another bite and motioned with his fork for her to do the same.

"Surprise?"

"You never know what's inside! Not unless you bite right in. *Empanadas* take commitment. A mouthful will tell."

"That's what you do, Claudio! You bite right in."

He nodded, smiled. "I commit."

Cover Our Inadequacy

Trinidad Méndez always had a boyfriend, so when she moved to New York City, her family and friends either hardly dared imagine, or imagined long and lustily, the exciting and dangerous men she would meet there. This same family and these friends welcomed her back with a sense of relief rather than a haughty "I told you so." Even Ken refrained from saying the words, though his smile held a certain smugness. He appeared at her door soon after she settled in, prepared to resume his role as sweetheart, as though time and distance had never parted them.

Trini was amused. She hadn't actually made up her mind to take Ken back, but it was easier to go out with him than to wrestle the relationship question, and what was her hurry anyway? No one seemed to think it odd to see the two back together – nobody but an obscure person whose opinion was hardly germane. To BOB, the pair posed as unlikely a combination as a rock and a rose, a thorn bush and a silk scarf, a robin's egg and a hammer.

Ken had graduated from university with an engineering degree, so he wasn't stupid; he was destined for success in his family's construction business, so he wasn't without prospects. But he was also fantastically rigid, so he wasn't indomitable either. There was something about playing by the rules that BOB felt sure he could use to make his point. He had to find some way to prove to Trinidad that Ken would never appreciate the beauty of her soul, and to settle for this would be tragic.

BOB was considering how best to conquer the magnificent obstacle presented by Ken, when he remembered something he had said to Carlos recently: "You can't win if you don't play." There was one area in which BOB excelled – the curious and capricious arena of the "self-invented game."

BOB delighted in concocting one game after another; challenging himself in contests of chance, skill, and intellect. He used his stores of knowledge: names of animals, herbs, plants, planets and continents; minerals, rocks, people, living and dead; generals, battles, economies and gross national products, to test himself continuously. People said he was amusing. They also called him weird. He didn't care – he was smart. They had to admit he was smart.

BOB thought of all this as he waited at Trini's house for her brother, Carlos. They were to play a game of war. BOB's variation of the game was one in which the stakes could be re-arranged or traded so that one would be vanquishing his foe one minute and flailing helplessly against him the next. BOB sat in the living room, in front of the old coffee table, shuffling through a Sears catalogue from last Christmas.

He sensed Trini's approach before she appeared. The air was charged, clean and clear, like a breeze before rain. He inhaled sharply.

"Looking for Carlos?"

He nodded. "Yeah."

"He should be back soon. Just ran down to the Shop-N-Save for Mamá."

BOB picked up a yellow legal pad that had been under the catalogue. "Hey, how 'bout a game?"

"Oh, thanks BOB but Ken should be here any minute."

BOB snorted.

"What?"

"Nothing." A pause, "Ken?"

"It's a name!"

"A short one."

"So's BOB!"

"No, I meant the game. A short game."

"Oh." Trini walked over to the window. She peered down the driveway. No sign of a car yet. "What kind of game?"

"War?"

"That's short?"

"Okay. 'What If?'"

"Another BOB original?"

"What if it is? Chicken?"

She crossed her arms. "Go on."

"What if you're...?" He looked about the room for clues. Books and more books, a cluttered desk, a sewing basket, a Girl Scout sash, waiting for its little badges to be sewn on, probably belonging to María Elena. BOB remembered María Elena teasing Trini because she didn't get any of the swimming badges – she was afraid of water! "...in a life boat."

Trini hid a smile. She looked the other way.

With his large eyes shining, BOB spoke softly, drawing her in. "What if you have with you your five most precious possessions? Here." He ripped a page from the legal pad, tore it in half and fished a pencil from his pocket. "Write them down."

She sat. "People?"

"If you like. Don't bother to write your own name. You're the one in the boat, after all." It didn't take her long to scribble five things. "The water is rough, getting rougher. A big wave washes over you, washes something overboard. Cross out the third thing on your list."

She frowned. "Okay." BOB's gravity made her uneasy.

"The day drags on. The sun beats down mercilessly. You're thirsty. Really thirsty. Your throat is parched, your tongue thick with fear. You'd kill for even a sip of water."

"Or a cigarette?"

"No. No joking. You want water! Check out what's left. What if I trade you the last thing on your list? For water?"

"How much water?" she murmured.

He raised an eyebrow. "A cup."

Trini shook her head.

"A gallon?"

"And how long do you think that would last?"

"What if I give you enough for, say, I don't know – a week?"

"Ugh. After a week without a shower I'm gonna wish I was dead anyway!"

"You and whoever you have on that list!"

Trini laughed. Her laugh was so beautiful it gave BOB a stabbing pain, and at the same time made him smile. Trini checked the window again. Nothing.

"Okay." She looked up. "Water!" She crossed something out with a flourish.

"Man, you're tough!'"

"What if you get in a boat, BOB?"

"What if I get in yours?"

"What if you already are?" But the way she said it, made it clear that he was not.

"Ha!" BOB coughed. "Okay, okay. Now, what if it's night and a storm brews up again? It's dark and you're wet, cold, freezing cold! You gotta get warm! You're scared to death and all you can think about is sweaters and down blankets and warm socks, and then suddenly – the boat springs a leak! You're going down!" He paused. "Holy shit – that's right – you can't swim!"

Trini white-knuckled her pencil. She forgot about checking the window. She whispered, "And?"

"And to keep afloat," he leaned forward slightly, "what if you have to toss one of the three items left?"

"I choose it?"

He nodded.

"But BOB, I can't do that. I don't like this game."

"It's not about liking. It's about making choices."

"BOB, it's just a game."

"Trini," he answered, "it's just a game."

She took a deep breath and crossed out one more thing.

"Okay now, hand me the pencil." She did. He closed his eyes and slashed through one of her remaining items.

"Hey!"

"Clumsy Coast Guard."

She smiled. "Well, at least he..."

"Don't tell me what's left." BOB smoothed the other half of the yellow paper and poised his hand to write. "My turn. Go."

"Okay." Trini folded up her decimated scrap of paper and kept it tucked in her fist. She eyed her opponent. "What if you're on an airplane?"

BOB smiled at his pencil. *"Touché!"* His fear of flying was a joke among those who knew him. Carlos was just complaining that if BOB wouldn't fly he couldn't film anything on location and sooner or later that was gonna be a problem. BOB said future problems have future solutions and Carlos said you can't just be existential when it's convenient for you. Trini overheard the whole thing.

"Little tiny tin can of a plane with two propellers and one is going out. You've got four things with you." She nodded at the paper.

"Only four?"

Trini shrugged. "Small plane. Plus, I figure you probably only own about four things."

"Ooh, cold!" BOB scribbled in silence. "Hey, wait, I just thought of one more. Don't worry. It won't take up any space." He wrote again. "Okay, go."

"Headwinds. Toss two."

"Two? Do you even know what a headwind is?" She laughed again.

"Brutal!" BOB chewed the end of his pencil. "Two," he muttered. Slowly, he drew a line through one thing and then more quickly, through another. He kept his eyes on his scrap of paper. "Go on."

"Okay, you're headed for a mountain top. Whoops! Good flying! You missed it but, oh no! A giant pterodactyl is coming straight at you, so in a panic, you grab the biggest thing left and fling it straight at the giant bird's head!"

"You know," BOB looked up, "this isn't a joke." He frowned at the paper, moved his hands like he was weighing something and slashed his list again. "Okay."

"Now, there's hardly anything left of your plane." Trini sounded sad. "I have a parachute. What will you trade me for it?"

"Oh, shit. Hey, what if I have one on the list?"

"Do you?"

"No."

"You have to live. To win."

"I know, I know. Shit." He crossed off one last thing. "Okay. Now, since I started the game, I get to make the offer." BOB stood. "I'll trade my last thing for yours. If you don't trade me, you only get one more day to live, but you get to keep your thing. Is it a deal?"

"No." She stood too, hands on hips, mouth set in a line.

"Hey, Trini! I've been sitting in the driveway for ten minutes! Didn't you see the car?" Ken suddenly filled the room.

"Ken!" She spun around. "You're here. I was just finishing a game with my friend, BOB."

BOB noticed she didn't say *my brother's friend*. "How's it goin', man?" BOB stuck out his hand. His crumpled list was still in it.

"What the hell's this?" Ken uncurled the paper and read aloud, "Universal Omnipotence? Exactly what game were you guys playing?"

"Oh, you wouldn't know it." BOB waved dismissively.

"More importantly," Ken pressed on, "who won?"

In unison they answered, "I did." Now they glared at each other. "No, I did!"

"But you're dead!" BOB insisted.

"Not yet, my friend!" Trini was surprised at her own vehemence.

"Trini, who cares?" Ken looked at his watch. "So what's the deal?"

"She could have had my omnipotence!" BOB sputtered. "Instead she chose to die for whatever's left on her list!"

"I won!" Trini protested, unfolding her proof. "He may rule the rest of the world, but he doesn't rule me! He couldn't take the thing I value most."

"Something you're willing to die for? Lemme see." Ken took her paper and read his own name. He hooted. "You could've had the world and you kept me instead?"

"You sound surprised." (Actually, Trini sounded that way.)

"Little fool! You could have gotten me back with worldly omnipotence!" He kissed her on the mouth.

Trini didn't return the kiss. "I didn't think that was an option."

"You mean you didn't think of it."

She blanched. "I didn't need to."

"Well, I guess that's why I'm the..." ("Ass," thought Trini, glancing at BOB and seeing the same thought reflected in his eyes.)... "engineer and you're the angel."

"You know the great thing about engineers?" BOB murmured. "They're really good at fixing things. For other people." He turned to Trini and raised an eyebrow. "You knew I'd win."

She had the feeling (she didn't know why) he wasn't talking about *What If.*

Forgive Us The Sin Of Loving One Another Too Much

"Trinidad! Carlitos! Come now. We will be late."

Mamá rarely raised her voice. There were only two things that could rouse such passion in her, and courtesy to God was one. "María Elena, where is your hat?" Hats must be worn on Sunday, especially on this Sunday and the next.

ME flew out the kitchen door, straw boater in one hand, prayer book in the other. Trailing behind her parents, she was halfway up the hill before Trinidad and Carlos caught up. Trini was combing her hair with her fingers and Carlos still buttoning his shirt. ME squinted at Trini. "You look like you just rolled out of bed."

"Thank you for noticing."

"You dress like lightning!" Carlos muttered.

"Is that a compliment?" ME asked.

"Why does it take you so long?" Trini answered.

"Oh, I don't know. Because I trouble to put on underwear?" Carlos raised an eyebrow as he straightened his shirtsleeves and finished buttoning his cuffs. ME clapped her hand over her mouth.

"Shut up!" Trini laughed.

Mamá pressed her lips together as everyone squeezed into the old Plymouth.

Once settled, Carlos jerked his chin toward their parents in the front seat. He murmured, "They should just be glad we still go to church."

"Amen!" Trini whispered. They suppressed their laughter.

Mamá turned around in her seat. She frowned at what she could see of Trini. "Is that how you dress to meet your Savior, Trinidad?"

Trini blinked. "Mamá, I'm not dying. We're just going to Mass."

"Just going to Mass?" Her mother's eyes were like two knives. With a harrumph, she turned back to glare at the road.

It was a short drive to the church. Trini always figured you could leave at noon to be at noon Mass. It was that close. Or she cut it that close.

"Trinidad," her father grabbed Mamá's hand as he spoke.

"Yes, Dad?"

"Going to Mass is never just going to Mass. It is the most important thing you will do all day. All week."

"Yes, Dad."

The silence was thick.

"How's BOB?" Carlos stirred the pot quietly, slyly.

Trini smiled at her folded hands. "You know. He's BOB."

Carlos nodded. "Funny, how you two hit it off. I mean, he's so – uncomfortable – around most people."

"Yeah."

"Not us though!" ME crossed her arms with purpose.

Trini smiled at her. "At first I thought it was just curiosity..."

"On your part or his?" Carlos teased.

"Trinidad?" Mamá was speaking to her again.

"Yes, Mamá?"

"Bring your new friend around for supper. After Mass. That boy's too skinny."

"Yes, Mamá."

"Your new friend?" ME pulled the brim of her hat down over her eyes.

The windows of the church were open, letting the first smell of thawed ground and new shoots blend with the heavy perfume of the female worshipers. Easter would be early this year; next week already. Trini was glad she had decided on bare feet and loafers instead of panty hose and pumps. Her father was in a suit and her mother wore her best long-sleeved dress and stockings. Little ME had on a good Sunday dress, her wide-brim straw hat now pinned to her head. They dressed for the occasion, not for comfort. Even Carlos was wearing a tie.

Trini sank back against the smooth wooden pew and tried to concentrate. The Passion was long and strangely clinical this year. (Perhaps it was the familiarity?) Until they got to the part about Barabbas, and then something troubled Trini – something about Barabbas.

When the crowd was given a choice to free innocent Jesus or the hardened criminal Barabbas, this year, like every year, they chose the criminal, and for the first time ever, Trini questioned what she would have done. She'd always blandly assumed she'd have had the guts to be different, to stand up for Jesus, to save God. Safely ensconced in the future, it was easy to declare confidence in making the right choice. But would she have chosen Jesus back then? She looked over at Carlos. Would he? One thing was sure. BOB would have had the courage to do the right thing. The thought quickened her heartbeat and shaped her lips into a smile.

"Just come over and eat. It's no big deal." Trini wound the long cord of the kitchen phone around her elbow. She could feel BOB's reluctance, hear him squirm. She chuckled. "Not because it's Palm Sunday. It's not like we're gonna expect you to ride in on a white donkey or anything. Just come. Mamá will be offended if you don't."

BOB weighed the relative discomfort of driving out to the sticks, in the middle of a Sunday, just to be cross-examined by a hoard of round-eyed inquisitive people bent on feeding him until his sides burst, against the kindness of Trini, his first, his only ever girlfriend. He rubbed the crease between his brows. "Okay."

"I'll keep ME away from you if that's what you're worried about."

"What? You're gonna drag me all the way out there only to desert me and leave me to fend for myself among..."

"No, no. Not me. ME. María Elena."

"Oh. No. Don't worry about her. I kind of get a kick out of her. Don't you?"

"Oh, well sure. But I have to. She's my sister."

BOB laughed. "Man, you guys are weird!"

She liked his laugh, sweet relief. "BOB, you're very brave." *Yes,* she thought, *he would have taken the heat for Jesus.*

BOB drove a Volkswagen Rabbit. He called it the VR. He wasn't making a statement against the consumption of gasoline (the VR ran on diesel fuel) and he wasn't trying to be different. He knew the guy who was selling it and he could afford it, that's all. But he was pleased that it allowed others to think of him as one who cared about the state of the world and who took an active stand for the environment.

BOB hummed Beethoven's Seventh Symphony as he made his way up the long dirt driveway. He saw Trini emerge from the house and he watched her run up the hill before he got out of the VR. He liked her graceful movements, the way she smoothed her hair when she reached him, like she thought he cared about how she looked.

He touched her shoulder by way of a greeting. "Hello, Trinidad."

"Hi!" Trini was out of breath. She leaned against the car, her breasts heaving slightly. She rubbed her palms together. This always came as a surprise to BOB, that he could make a girl nervous. He grabbed her hands and moved forward, standing between her legs.

"So-o-o..." He grinned.

"Now, don't get any ideas," she scolded him. "You're here to eat and get fat and healthy and relaxed."

"Don't be silly. I wouldn't know how to relax!" His gaze pierced her like granite pressing into something soft.

She blushed. "H-How's the story coming?"

BOB actually winced. As if changing his mind, he laughed instead. "The one I'm reading or the one I'm writing?"

"Ha. I don't think I'd call *War and Peace* a story. I meant the one you're writing."

"Everything's a story, Trini. And I'm slogging through both." He kept his eyes locked on hers and pressed forward slightly. She smelled the warm fragrance of his skin, took in the small freckles at the corners of his eyes, the way his bangs fell unevenly across his forehead, the determined line of his chin. Mesmerized, she forgot they were standing in the driveway in the sun, until Mamá broke the spell by calling them.

Two hours later they were back in the driveway, this time Trini letting BOB kiss her goodbye. "This meant a lot to me. Thanks for coming," she said.

"Well, you mean a lot to me."

The meal had been two hours of torture and triumph, BOB taking full possession of his new-boyfriend status, and along with it, making him self a natural target for Carlos' wit. Trini's gentle acquiescence and patience with her brother made Carlos' barbs seem inconsequential, childish even. The realization of this introduced BOB to a new guilty pleasure. He actually felt pity for his friend.

BOB took quite a leap when he elevated himself from weird friend of Carlos to Trinidad's dependable beau. Everyone thought so, though nobody said a word.

Trini ran back down to the kitchen as the VR took off with a lurch. Carlos was standing in front of the sink, back to the window, hands on his hips.

"What?" Trini said.

"What what?" came the obtuse reply.

"Okay, what did I do to piss you off?"

"Who says I'm pissed off?"

"Why else would you be such a jerk to your best friend and your favorite sister?"

"Oh, ho! My favorite?"

"You know what I mean."

"And you know what you did."

"What?"

"You changed him."

"What? Who?"

Carlos thought of all the late-night foreign films he and BOB would not be seeing anymore. He thought about the way they used to stand in a bar afterwards engrossed in heated arguments about art, drinking Cokes, disdaining all the women who wouldn't talk to them. Those things would all be lumped together now under the heading of *what we did before BOB met Trinidad*. "He's not BOB anymore, that's all."

"Oh, Carlitos! He's just not your BOB anymore." She went to the sink, started filling it with sudsy water. "He's not really my BOB either, you know. It's not – he's not – like that."

Carlos made a face, but Trini didn't see. She was watching another car coming up the driveway. It was Ken's Datsun, blue, like his eyes.

Tall and robust, Ken knocked at the screen door and smiled too broadly at Mamá. "Hello, Mrs. Méndez! These are for you." He handed her lilies, pure white with waxy fragrance.

"Thank you, Ken! Please come in. Have you eaten yet?"

"Thanks, ma'am. My mother has Sunday dinner a little later. I'm fine right now. Is Trini around?"

"Trinidad! You have a visitor."

Trini and Carlos were hidden from view, listening in the seclusion of the staircase. Now Trini smoothed her hair and bit her lips on her way to the kitchen. "Yes, Mamá?" She managed a look of surprise. "Why, Ken! How nice."

He leaned over and kissed the cheek she quickly offered, stifling a laugh. "Hello, Trini."

"Let's go outside."

"Sure."

She led him through the house to the front door and outside to the porch swing. It was chilly now. Trini shivered as she sat.

"Here you go." Ken wrapped his sweater around her shoulders and then added his arm for good measure. "You know, you haven't been very...well...very nice to me lately. Are we fighting?"

She blinked. "Are you kidding me?"

"Hardly."

"Ken, how do you not...?" She lowered her voice and continued. "Let me put it to you this way: I thought I made it perfectly clear. You and I don't have a future. And I'm not so crazy about our present either."

"What do you mean?"

"Ken, I told you, it's o..."

She didn't get the word out before he covered her mouth with his. And he didn't let her up for air until he'd hurt her neck with his penetrating kiss.

An hour later, Trini was putting the last of the leftovers away while Mamá wiped the counter. "So, I keep wondering what I would have done," Trini said. "If I lived back then."

"Don't be silly, Trinidad," her mother gently chided. "You are human. You would have chosen Barabbas."

The comfortable conversation between the two women twisted into barbed wire. "What did you say, Mamá?" Had she seen Ken kissing her? Trini was so surprised at first, she couldn't move. Finally, she turned toward her mother

"Of course you would have. You do it now."

"I choose Barabbas?"

Her mother nodded. "You do."

"But, Mamá! I have integrity. I speak up. I'm honest."

"Are you?"

Trini didn't know what to say. She thought she lived honorably. She had settled the question of love and sex long ago. Okay, she'd made a mistake with Ken. Turned out that wasn't love at all, but how did she know? How could she tell at the time?

"Mamá, I do my best..."

"Trinidad, you don't even know what your best is yet." Mamá went on wiping the counter, making little circles with the dishrag. "We all choose Barabbas. Every day. Every time we perform some little task without giving it our best effort, we put something before God. We choose Barabbas. When we run in late to Mass, leave a little early, plan our workday while listening to a friend in need; when we give just a little to the poor so that it does not really inconvenience us – we choose Barabbas."

"But Mamá, you never choose Barabbas. You don't put anything before God!"

Mamá looked out the window, over the field where Trini's father was walking, testing the ground to see if it was too wet to mow. A little stiff now, bow legged, but still handsome; he wore a hat to cover the balding spot on his head. She smiled a small secret smile. "Oh, *Querida*," Mamá said softly, "I am human too." She drew in a breath, shook her head. "At one time or another in our poor lives, we all choose Barabbas."

Allow Us To Trust In Your Greater Plan For Our Welfare

María crouched behind the fence, next to her big sister, bare toes curled into the dirt. Rafaela put a finger to her lips.

"I can't see," María whispered.

"Here," Rafaela pulled her closer and pointed to a gap between the boards.

When she looked now, she saw two neighbor boys, brothers, with a lovely gray mule. The older boy straddled the mule and both brothers were clucking and using a stick, trying to get the mule to do something. "Such a pretty mule! Are they teaching it a trick?"

Rafaela giggled. "Ah, *sí*! The mule bolts sharply to the left each time Manuel uses his heels. *Mira?*"

When the mule hesitated, Oziel urged it on with a sharp blow. María angrily leaped to her feet. She wouldn't stand by watching, while those boys hit a poor beast!

"Sh! Get down!" Rafaela yanked her back to the ground.

In the distance they heard, "Eh! Manuel, Ozielito! Bring out the mule. Tío Tomás is waiting!"

The girls' cheeks bulged and their faces grew red with the effort to keep from laughing. The boys called out "*Sí*, Papá!" and whispered furiously to one another.

"Do you think he will do it?" Ozielito squinted in the bright sun, his head cocked to one side.

"Ah, *sí.* He is a smart mule," Manuel answered, slipping from his back and grinning. He took something from his pocket for the mule and scratched him between his long, bristly ears.

The sun made the horizon shimmer with little ripples of heat. Tío Tomás strode into the stable yard, muttering in Spanish, shooing the boys away. He heaved himself onto the mule's back and yanked its head to face the road. The mule obeyed as always, but when his master clucked and tapped his heels against its sides, the beast bolted sharply to the left, thrusting the ponderous Tomás from its back, and onto the hard ground. The girls jumped up and screamed, then clapped their brown hands to their mouths and took off at a run.

In a rage, Tomás leapt to his feet and grabbed each boy by the ear. Amid expletives was a very real promise that they'd live to regret whatever it was they had done to his mule. Tío Tomás dragged them off for a proper beating. Ozielito was crying already, but Manuel looked with interest after the fleeing neighbor girls. Chest puffed out; he was still grinning. He would endure the beating, and though the tears might flow down his cheeks, he would not make a sound.

That night María had trouble sleeping. When she closed her eyes she saw the mule, his great eyes rolling in his head, blood-shot and full of fear. María rolled over. She kicked the blankets away, pressed her fists into her own eyes. *Oh, no!* Two red dots, sentinels, appeared at the far corners of her sight and floated determinedly front and center. She pressed her lips together. She knew them. Her stomach knotted in a ball. Two more dots soon followed those, then two more, four, then eight. Soon they had become a whole sea of red dots, slowly crowding out the familiar shadows of the room before rising in a great wave to the ceiling. María pulled the blankets up and over her head and whimpered.

"What is it?" Rafaela whispered. "*Los puntos*?"

María mutely nodded, a small lump under the quilt. She couldn't see her sister smile.

"Don't be frightened. They are not monsters. Don't they look like small jewels, little sparkles? Like the necklaces we put on the Virgin Mary for May Crowning?"

She heard a mumbled "No. Those are made of flowers."

"Ah, *sí*," Rafaela murmured. "Still, they are pretty, aren't they?"

The covers were flung back suddenly and María sat up. "You see them, too? The dots?"

"Oh," Rafaela waved her hands in the dark. "I used to see them all the time. The trick is to make them your friends. Then, poof! They disappear until you need them again."

"But I don't need them now."

"You do if you fear them. They don't wish to be feared."

María closed her eyes again. There they were, small, winking red. They did sparkle. She watched them float up to the ceiling, wave upon wave of small red dots, like tiny fish, flower petals, the snowflakes Papá told them he'd seen as a boy. But those were white, weren't they? Still, Rafaela was right. They were friendly. And they sparkled...and...and... She slept at last.

Years later, when Manuel wed Rafaela, he would recount the mule story as the first time he ever noticed his wife's grace, her beauty, long legs and pigtails flying. Little María was more of a blur, he'd laugh, quicker than her sister and already far in the distance. This story made both girls proud, but María secretly wished she could have been the graceful one, instead of only fast.

The two sisters were often together, even after Rafaela married Manuel and moved into his mother's house. "María is my other half. When you get one, you get both," Rafaela used to say, as if such an explanation were necessary.

"Ah, two riches. *¡Dos tesoros por el precio de uno!*" he would reply.

María bit her lip. She knew one day she would have to marry, but she despaired of ever finding the happiness her sister enjoyed.

"Manuel is so funny!" Rafaela laughed. "Do you know how he woke me this morning? He shook a bunch of flowers in my face! They were still wet with dew and when I scolded him he said, 'The poor flowers are jealous of your beauty, Love. Don't blame them for crying.'"

María looked down. She blushed, picturing her sister and Manuel in their clean, simple bedroom. "You never were an early riser," she answered.

"Ah, not like you, to be sure. You are always up before the sun. You and Manuel."

"Then it must be true that opposites attract."

"And that must be why I love you both!"

Rafaela was lighthearted, carefree. She liked to sleep late, spend her days sewing and dreaming, while María preferred harder work. She gardened, cooked and cleaned, finding satisfaction in a window so clear it looked as though it held no glass, or a meal of hearty stew with an overflowing tortilla basket.

Manuel and Rafaela had only been married a few months when Rafaela complained of fatigue.

Her mother-in-law nodded, slyly, happily. "It's about time! Yes, yes, marriage is like that."

Rafaela bit her lip.

But the next week her period started. She cried and cried. Everyone tried to comfort her.

"Oh, it's nothing. Don't be so delicate, dear. These things work themselves out." Rafaela's mother-in-law was beating a rug with a wire brush, the dust making her sneeze.

But the bleeding didn't stop. Rafaela's fatigue became a pale inability to rise, a fever that would not abate. The bliss with which her marriage started soon turned to concern. As Rafaela grew weaker, María couldn't help noticing how strong Manuel appeared. He was like her, sturdy and hardworking.

Manuel wanted the doctor, but he was a *gringo*, both too far away and too expensive. A *gringo* doctor would not travel to see a woman, a Mexican woman, with female complaints. They knew this and accepted it as natural, redoubling their prayers. Rafaela went to bed with strong tea and mustard plasters to draw away the infection.

One day María made *empanadas*. She brought a plate of them to her sister's house. Manuel opened the door.

"Manuel, you must eat something. You cannot both fall ill."

"Ah, you sound like my mother." His voice had a sudden catch in it.

"What is it?" María asked hurriedly. "Is she worse?"

He shook his head. "Mother." He swallowed. "It's just a word, I know, but Rafaela is heart-broken that she may never...this illness... I tell her it doesn't matter, that we have years to..."

María swallowed. Rafaela must be worse. She shoved the plate toward him and turned to go so that he wouldn't see the tears in her eyes.

"Wait. Wait," he grabbed her wrist and felt her warm brown skin, her muscles tense, life flowing, churning through her veins. He quickly let go. "I mean, thank you. I'll give her an *empanada*. If she would only eat..."

"I'll take one to her." María smoothed her hair and took the plate from him again. She saw that he needed her.

She made her way to the bedroom with one *empanada* and a cup of clear broth. Manuel's mother whisked her through the spotless kitchen and the elegant dining room, making little clucking noises at the thought that María would try to feed her sister a meat pie when what she needed was broth. She should have known better!

María could not believe how thin and frail Rafaela looked, lying in the middle of her double bed. Her sister smiled weakly at the fragrant *empanada*. She wrinkled her nose at the broth. "Now, you must try at least one bite. I spent all morning making them. Of course they won't be as good as yours, but still..." María set the small dish on a table next to the bed. She helped her sister to sit up and fluffed the pillow behind her, straightened the blanket. Then she busied herself about the room, dusting a chair, moving the curtains, straightening an embroidery frame.

Rafaela took a tiny bite and sighed with pleasure. "It's delicious. You've become a very good cook." She spoke softly.

"What?" María sat on the edge of the bed. "Is it okay?"

Rafaela nodded. She laid one hand on her sister's. "You must promise me something." Her face was placid, as though the request were a simple one.

"Of course," María said automatically.

Rafaela took so long to continue that María thought perhaps she was too tired to talk. "You have to take care of him. For me."

María's heart beat painfully. She frowned. "I don't know what...don't be silly! You're getting stronger every day. Why by next summer..."

Rafaela shook her head slowly. "Please. For me."

María felt a tingling that went from her belly to her head. Her face burned. How she longed to do just that! Shame immediately consumed her. "You will get better," she said firmly, vowing to herself that she would not quit petitioning the Lord until this happened. Distress at the cruelty of her own fate would fuel her pleas. Rafaela could live in happiness if only she would continue to live, and María would offer up her own unhappiness as a sacrifice.

Later that day, as María left, she passed through the dining room. Manuel sat at the table, the remaining *empanadas* in front of him, untouched. She longed to smooth his hair, to offer what comfort she could. Such longing bound her hands, hushed her voice, and she could only hurry by. A sob escaped when she reached the door and suddenly Manuel was at her side. He pulled her close with one hand and with the other, patted her back. "Sh, sh, María. She says it is as God wills. We must be strong."

María clung to him then, misery shaking her small frame. Oh, if he knew why she cried, he would think her selfish, cruel, a monster. She nodded and pulled away. "I have to go home, Manuel," she choked. And off she ran.

But she returned the next day and the next. She sat with her sister, read to her, told her funny stories about the chickens or the goat. Most of it she made up, but it didn't matter. She'd say anything to make her sister smile.

"Ah, you're here!" Manuel always welcomed her. His face would light up briefly, and even though she knew it was only because his wife would not be alone, his eagerness lifted her spirits, made her feel her presence counted for something.

Rafaela slept little and fitfully. María placed a wet cloth on her forehead when the fevers came; rubbed her arms, her hands and feet for chills. When Manuel moved into another room, María took to sleeping in a chair, next to her sister's bed.

"You don't mind?" Rafaela whispered to María.

"Mind? Of course not. It's like when we were girls. I never sleep well alone; you know that," María insisted, keeping her eyes on her embroidery.

One night María saw her sister smiling with her eyes closed. "Rafaela," she whispered, "Are you awake?"

Rafaela nodded, still smiling, her face white in the moonlight. "They're back," her voice came faint and small.

"Who's back?"

"They want to take me with them," she said. "I shall be a tiny floating dot, like them – a sparkle, a little star."

María grabbed her sister's hand. "No, Rafaela, no! Don't go."

"You must not fear, María."

Her sister sobbed. "Stay here with me. Who will love me when you're gone?"

Rafaela's eyes opened slowly. In them María read the words, *you know*. And when she closed them again, it was for the last time.

Granting Strength And Patience
To Resist What Is Not Ours

"Mamá, does God have a birthday?"

"No sweet girl. He always was."

"What do you mean?"

"God wasn't born, Trinidad. He was always there."

"Was heaven always there too?"

"No. Just God. He is what is."

"Then when does God get presents?"

"Every time you're kind to someone, God gets a present."

"No, I mean, like, when does He get money? He could give it to the poor and then they could have presents too."

"God has nothing to do with money. God's gift is love. When we love one another, when we're generous to one another, we share in God's love, and He spreads that love to the poor all over the world, to people who are starving, living in dirt, so they can be happy even though they have nothing, because love is the most important thing there is. God's love."

"The most important thing there is..." Trini murmured.

"Now, stop looking for cherries in the snow, Love. It's past your bedtime." Mamá pulled the blankets up to her little one's chin and turned out the light.

Trini was seven years old. She wasn't as pious as Adela, nor as beautiful as Modesta, never as strong or as fast as her brothers, Nunzio and Carlos. But she was curious. She was thoughtful. And once determined upon her path, she never gave up.

Trinidad Méndez did well in school. She pleased her teachers and was kind to the other students. Along with the rest of her female classmates, Trini had now joined the ranks of girls becoming women. Tender breasts had finally appeared, mirrored by the curve of her hips. She took great care of her hair, curling it, making it shine. She was slowly ripening, innocently alluring, attractive without the con- sciousness that gives women power.

Of course the boys instinctively responded and the more experienced ones turned their attention to capturing a prize. "Yo, Trini, man. Nice sweater."

She blushed.

"Hey, save me a seat, will ya?"

"I'm on my way to Home Ec!" She scurried away.

"Yo! You can sit on my lap, Princess."

Princess? That's what they used to call Modesta!

The hunt was on and the quarry remained blissfully ignorant, aware only that the boys had finally noticed her. Trinidad Méndez had arrived!

By the time she was a high school senior, it was natural that Trini should be elected the first runner-up for homecoming queen. The queen was a cheerleader named Bobbi – one who surely deserved the title, wealthy, blonde, plus she'd had a figure since the fifth grade.

"First runner-up, eh?" Her brother, Nunzio, teased. "I wonder how close it was?"

Carlos looked up from his book. "I heard she lost by only one vote."

Trini was startled. "One?" she echoed.

"What's the difference?" Nunzio was lacing up his work boots. "Nothing you can do about it. I mean, it's not like you didn't vote for yourself or anything!"

Ah, but it was.

Trinidad told herself she'd rather be first runner-up anyway. She didn't have a dress for the dance yet, or even a date! How embarrassing would it have been to be crowned queen without an attending king?

One morning, a Saturday morning, Trini's mother found her sitting at the kitchen table, her head in her hands.

"*Querida*, you are up early." Trini nodded. Her mother busied herself around the kitchen, brewing coffee, chopping peppers and onions for the eggs. Trini sighed. Her mother stopped, knife mid-air. "Already looking for cherries in the snow?"

"Mamá, this is real. Tony asked me to the prom last night."

"How nice." Silence. "Isn't it?"

"Well, yes, I guess so. But David asked me too. He asked me first."

"And?"

"And I told him I would let him know because I really want to go to the prom, but I was hoping Ken would ask me and then Tony goes and does and I couldn't tell him I'd let him know too, so I said no, but I'd rather go with Tony than with David. And the person I really want to go with is Ken."

"*Querida*, you make everything so complicated!"

"I do?"

"Yes, you do. It was a simple question after all."

"But Mamá, what if Ken never asks me? What if Tony and David are the only ones who do and if I say no to both of them I can't go to the prom at all! And I hate hurting either of them, let alone both of them! But I'll never please them both. I can't please everyone!"

"Trinidad! You are confusing the issue. There is only one person you must please!'"

"I know, I know," she said, resigned. "Myself."

Her mother stiffened. "Certainly not! You must please God." Trini blinked. "You were honest with Tony. Be honest with David as well." Her mother smothered a chuckle as she broke eggs into a dish.

"Mamá, it's not funny!"

"The truth seldom is."

So Trini did the hard thing, the honest thing, and turned down both boys. By the time she discovered Ken would be out of town the weekend of the prom she had turned down a third offer as well.

Trini got, if not prettier, certainly more desirable as she matured, and eventually the question of her chastity began to trouble her. Was everyone else really doing it? What her mother called her crowning jewel no longer seemed a treasure to be cherished, but a weight that grew heavier each day. Finally, mostly from exhaustion, she threw it away on Ken just before graduation.

"C'mon Trini," Ken breathed into her hair. He moved a curl from her ear and gently licked.

She caught her breath. They were in his car, in a remote part of the park. The stars twinkled overhead and the Eagles were singing "Hotel California," and Ken's aftershave was so lovely, so strong and sophisticated smelling, so sweet...

"Don't you love me, Baby?" He shifted to a more comfortable position and pressed his lips onto hers so that she couldn't answer.

She squirmed. "Wait, wait."

He backed off and she sat up suddenly, her face glowing. Then she leaned over him, pressed into him and surprised him with a kiss of her own...

After this, the ability to please belonged to her, but Ken's easy assumption that this part of Trini really belonged to him, without any sacrifice or commitment on his part, offended her and left her feeling rather nettled.

Trini was happy and relieved when she made up her mind to move away. Distance would end the problem, allow her to clear her head, maybe gain a new perspective. But before she left, Trini decided to be generous to Ken one last time, an intimate goodbye, her going away present.

"Well," Ken was buttoning his shirt. "You want to go to the movies tomorrow night? *Star Wars* is at the drive-in."

Trini shook her head and then raked her fingers through the tangle of her curls. "You know I'm not crazy about sci-fi. Besides, I have to pack."

"What?" He sat next to her on the ground. They'd taken a walk on the golf course where Ken worked summers. It was a warm, sticky night. The sound of the bullfrogs around the pond on the eighth hole drowned out the crickets. "Where you goin'?"

"I told you!" Trini shook her head again. "You know, you're not a great listener."

"Hey, maybe I'm good at other things." He moved closer and kissed her full lips.

"Ha!" She kissed him back. "I'm gonna find my fortune, remember?"

He vaguely recalled her complaining a few weeks ago of boredom, routine, the predictability of living in the same place your whole life and how she needed a new adventure. Was that it? "So where do you start?"

"I'm moving to New York."

"City?"

She nodded. "Modesta has a friend there who's gonna help me find a job. Actually, he's gonna let me crash on his couch, which is huge, right?"

"*He* is?"

"It's nothing like that. Besides," she laughed, "Modesta doesn't have any female friends."

"Hmm." Ken chewed his lip.

"I can come home weekends and stuff, you know."

Ken leaned back and looked up at the stars. He knew this was his cue. Did he love her? He didn't love the foreign films, the Syrian restaurants she was always dragging him to. He wasn't happy about the constant scrutiny with which her family regarded him. When he envisioned his wife, he pictured a blonde, tall, wealthy, well educated, well built. She never looked like Trini.

But there was something special about her. He'd miss her laugh, her sympathetic eyes, her scent of coconuts and flowers. He touched her hand, still hesitating, when suddenly the sprinklers came on and they had to make a dash for the car.

Two days later, Trini left.

Ken was surprised to find himself wondering what Trini was doing, whom she might be spending time with. He never told anyone this startling revelation. When Trini moved back home, he waited until a full three days had passed, before casually showing up and resuming his role as boyfriend, expecting all of the privileges that went along with it.

And then Trini discovered she had feelings for BOB.

With a child-like sense of loyalty and bemusement, she immediately changed the rules. Now what was Ken to do? Palm Sunday had been something of a revelation to him, but he felt he'd handled what must have been feminine problems, and showed a unique understanding in doing so. She probably only needed more time; more time and more attention.

Trini had struggled to pull back from Ken's kiss on the porch swing. "Hey! What's wrong?" he sputtered.

"Ken, I, it's just..."

"Is it that time of the month?"

"No!" Trini rolled her eyes. "See, this is it. Sometimes I feel like you don't even know me! Everything's so simple for you, so predictable. It's like, you think you have it all figured out when you don't even know what you're talking about."

"Okay, okay. Then it's that other time of the month."

"What?"

"You know, that PMS crap. Stuff, I mean."

"No! You're not listening to me. I keep telling you..." Trini took a deep breath. "Ken, please, listen closely this time: it's over."

"Over? I have no idea what you're talking about. Look, if this is some ploy to make me propose, just calm down. I know that whole clock ticking thing..."

"Ken, stop trying to define the problem. This isn't something you can fix. Stop thinking like an engineer for a minute and be *a man*. I'm trying to tell you..."

"A man? You're questioning my manhood? I was quarterback our Senior Year! I won my college wrestling championship. And you're telling me I don't think like a man?"

"Oh, forget it. What I meant is, you are thinking like a man and it isn't helping."

"Hey, I'm not one of those touchy feely sensitive guys with long hair and a guitar. I thought you liked that about me."

"I did like that you're not annoying in that way, but it doesn't change the fact that in your own pig-headed way..."

"Okay, enough's enough." Ken stood. "You can call me when you're feeling better. I didn't drive over here to take abuse today. Not from you."

Trini didn't try to stop him. She just watched him walk away.

Ken drove to the lake (after all, it wouldn't look good if he returned home too early). He sat in his car, studying the people shuffling along the path in velour jogging suits. He shook his head. How did these people do it? Some of these geezers had to be married for a hundred years! And what was wrong with Trini anyway? It must be some female thing. He was her man – wasn't he?

Meanwhile, on the other side of town, in a run-down neighborhood where half the houses had been divided into rental units, BOB stood at a window, holding something up to the uncertain light. He could smell rather than feel the chilled air seeping through the space between the glass and the frame. He smiled, examining a small pebble, painted red. "Like cherries in the snow," he mused, turning it over in his hand.

And The Courage to Act Upon
Our Most Precious Convictions

BOB pulled into Trini's driveway, surprised to see the blue Datsun already in front of the barn. Ken got out of the Datsun and rose to his full height – 6 feet 3 inches. It was as if he'd been waiting for BOB to arrive.

"Hey, Bob, is it?" Ken stuck out a massive hand.

"Yeah." BOB shook it, miffed that his own was clammy.

"You here to see Carlos?"

That's right. He would remember I was Carlos' friend, forget that Trini had introduced me as her friend! "No."

Ken raised an eyebrow.

"Trini."

To BOB's surprise, Ken nodded and smiled.

Ken thought, *I knew it had to be something, but...this kid?* Ken snorted. "Let's go down, shall we?"

Mrs. Méndez watched the boys from her kitchen window. She laughed out loud.

"Mamá! What's so funny?"

"Oh, Papá! I was just remembering some-thing."

"What?"

"That story of the tortoise and the hare."

Papá came up behind her and put his arms around her waist. "That's not funny, *mi Amor!*" She laughed again. "I never said it was."

When they knocked, Papá answered the door.

"Mr. Méndez," BOB began.

"Is Trini home?" Ken asked quickly.

Papá sized up the situation, chuckled and cleared his throat. "I'm sorry, boys. Trinidad is not at home."

"Thank you, sir. I'll call her later. I was just in the neighborhood." Ken turned to go. He glanced back at BOB, still hesitating by the door.

"Mr. Méndez, would you give Trini something for me?" He fished in his pocket.

"Sure, Son." Trini's father smiled kindly at his nervousness. When BOB dropped two painted stones into his hand he looked puzzled.

"She'll understand," BOB said, turning back to the hill.

"What the hell was that?" Ken muttered, easily keeping pace with BOB's rapid gait.

"Message for Trini. Weren't you listening?"

"Look, don't be smart with me, Stick Man!"

"Stick Man?"

"Yeah, Sport. I don't have to tell you to stay away from Trini, do I?"

"You can if you want me to stay away from her, but it won't make any difference. You don't make the rules."

They were in the driveway, at the top of the hill now. Ken faced BOB with a menacing sneer. "You're crazy, you know that? You think she's even gonna consider leaving me in a million years? For you? You know what you are? You're just plain crazy!"

BOB smiled. "Then why so worried, Kenny?"

Ken clenched his fist, then slowly released it. "I swear to God... Look, I don't want to break your neck or anything, but I will if you go after her behind my back."

"Ditto."

"Hey, she's not your...and I'm not the kind of guy who sneaks around! I don't cheat. I don't have to."

"That's bullshit, man. You're cheating now. With my girl."

"Your what?"

"She's mine already. You don't know her; you don't care about her like I do."

Trini's words echoed uncomfortably in Ken's mind. *Sometimes I feel like you don't even know me.*

Ken remembered the first time he noticed Trini, one night at a field party, Junior Year. He'd asked one of his friends who she was.

"Trinidad Méndez? Man, you're dreaming!"

He watched her giggling with her friends. "What? You think I couldn't get a girl like that? A newbie, a virgin?"

His friend had laughed, slapped him on the back. "No, man, I don't. She's not just a prize, that one's got brains. And her family – you ever see her dad? And her brothers? Well, the big one, anyway..."

"Ha! I could take him."

"And you'd still have to convince her."

So naturally, he'd made it his business to win her. No one would tell him what he could and couldn't do!

Not then, not now. "Why, I oughta lay you out flat!"

"Go ahead." BOB shrugged. "That would help me a hell of a lot more than you."

Ken knew he was right. His mind automatically evaluated the situation, calculated what he could do to up the ante, how BOB would counter, then his maneuver, then BOB again – but ultimately, in a contest of superiority, it didn't matter what he had to offer so much as what Trini actually wanted...and lately, it wasn't him. It might not be this creep either, but it definitely wasn't him.. Stones? What was with the stones? Ken shrugged. He flung a half-hearted, "Go to Hell," at BOB, got in his car and drove off.

Later that night Trini's father knocked on her bedroom door. "Trinidad?"

"Yes, Dad? C'mon in."

He entered, looked around the little room that she shared with María Elena. He remembered when she shared the room with her two older sisters. Trini, Adela, and Modesta slept here, played here, occasionally fought here.

Trinidad had become a woman now, and such a woman that men were fighting over her. She looked up from the bed where she was laying on her stomach, with a book.

"What are you reading?"

"Oh, I'm just re-reading *Gone With The Wind*. Don't you wish life was still like that?"

"Gory and painful or painfully romantic?"

"Oh, Dad! Romantic of course!" She laughed.

"It still is, Love." He dropped the stones onto her book. "A message from your friend."

She stared at the stones, her heart beating. "What friend?"

He smiled. "The new one, of course."

"Of course," she echoed.

"He seemed to think you would understand."

María Elena burst into the room. "Hey Trini, Hey Dad. Trini, can I borrow your really red lipstick? You know the one?"

"You mean my good one?"

"Yeah. What's it called? I want to get one just like it."

Trini went to fetch her lipstick. She read the bottom of the tube aloud. "Cherries In The Snow. That's funny..."

"Wow." María Elena grabbed the lipstick from her. "Just like Mamá always says! Spooky, huh?"

Trinidad held the painted stones up to the overhead light. "So that's it..." She tingled with approval.

Wrapped in the Innocent and Candid Faith of Children

Golden filigree glowed softly in the candle-light. *If I believe God is really here, I will find rest in Him,* Manuel thought, genuflecting and taking his place close to the altar. It was First Friday again, what Rafaela had called Little Good Friday. "Every first Friday, Little Good Friday, every first Sunday, Little Easter." He smiled, remembering the way she would say it in her singsong voice. He felt himself alone, and yet not alone, in the darkened chapel lit only by the candles surrounding the Holy Eucharist. This marked the twelfth Exposition of The Holy Eucharist he attended without his beloved Rafaela.

Manuel prayed wordlessly for most of an hour, offering the ache in his heart as a sacrifice to Christ Jesus, an offering for her soul. Finally, he laid his head on his hands and whispered, "What am I to do, Lord? I still love her so much. As time passes, it does not hurt less. Why did she have to leave me?"

"She belonged to Me first."

He swallowed. Had somebody spoken or did he imagine it? He knew Rafaela was God's child, as was he, as was her sister. "Oh, Dear Lord, how can I take another? They say it is time." Manuel hid his face in his hands and stayed that way for a long while, a figure of misery and humility.

Finally, he looked up. He heard a small stifled sigh and glanced to his right. There he saw María kneeling next to him, her head bowed in prayer. When did she arrive? He'd heard nothing. She glanced at him, briefly raised her eyebrows. He gave a quick nod, noting the sense of relief that suddenly flooded him. As always, her presence was a comfort rather than an intrusion.

María returned to her prayers, watching Manuel from the corner of her eye, his rough hands folded, wide shoulders hunched a little. He made no sound, but soon pressed the back of his hand to his eyes, and turned to face her. María held her breath. Slowly he reached over and took her hand. He squeezed it, and she returned the pressure. They stayed like that, praying, until he gave her a questioning look.

When she nodded, he rose and drew her to her feet. They turned and both genuflected. He held the door for her and they stepped out into the dim light of late afternoon. "Shall I walk you home?" he asked.

"Not yet," she whispered.

"Shall we visit your sister, then?"

"Yes, please."

Manuel took María's arm. They walked behind the church, through the small cemetery and stopped at Rafaela's grave.

"I miss her," María said.

Manuel patted her arm. "As do I." Manuel cleared his throat. "María, I am...that is...I don't know when...I don't know if..."

"You don't?" Her heart beat painfully.

Manuel shook his head. "The tradition is a good one. It makes sense for many reasons, but when I give my heart and my life to you, it will not be because of tradition or to please the family, but because you are you, María, and I could do no less."

She looked hopeful now. He hadn't said he loved her, but he did value her. "Please Manuel, could we keep all this between ourselves until you are ready?"

He smiled at her delicacy, tucked a curl behind her ear. "A small secret, to be treasured?"

"Yes." María smiled too, relieved. "A treasure." She placed a flower on her sister's headstone and they walked to the gate. "Manuel," María said finally, "Have you been keeping First Friday all along?"

"Yes," he confessed. "It was so important to Rafaela, I didn't like to disappoint her."

"I, too, think of that."

"Of course." He smiled at her, and for the first time it occurred to him that he was looking at a woman, not just his wife's little sister. "And today I had a another purpose in mind. Today I had to beg our Father's assistance."

María's eyes grew big, but she didn't say a word.

"Child, naturally you will wear white! What else?"

María stood at the window, looking out. Her mother could tell her stubborn mindset by the crossed arms, the stiffness of her back in her good black dress. She didn't answer.

"You cannot wear black to your own wedding," Mamá said softly, laying a hand on that shoulder, so eager to take up the burdens of married life. "Rafaela would not like it."

"I don't know why we're even talking about this! He hasn't asked me and just because we took a walk..."

"You know, it is best to be ready."

María caught her breath, "But..."

"Rafaela wished you both to go on. Together. It is the nature of things." María remained staring out the window. She burned with shame. "Ah," Mamá smiled, "it is good to love your husband. If God has put that in your heart already it is His love that you bear – a sure sign."

María's face softened, her eyes wide. "Mamá, are you sure?" Her mother couldn't know that she had long loved Manuel. Long before her sister died, even before they wed...

"Ah, *sí*. It is His will. Now," María's mother went briskly to the cupboard and pulled out the white dress that Rafaela had worn for her own wedding, the one she, herself wore years ago, "let's see what we must do to make this fit."

"No, Mamá, no. I cannot put on her dress. It is too soon."

"Nonsense! It has been more than a year!" Mamá drew her daughter to the bed and smoothed her hair. "You do her no dishonor by honoring her wish."

"But I told you, he hasn't even asked me yet!"

"María! It will not hurt. Now, just for me then, try it on. After all, I will need time to make the alterations."

María was shorter than Rafaela had been, and more round. She stepped into the frothy white gown Mamá held out and pulled the sleeves into place. She held her breath while Mamá tried to button it. "We'll just move these over," Mamá muttered, "let this out. There's a good two inches left here and here." She tugged and pinned and even though there was no mirror, it was an effort for María to keep from smiling. Her wedding. Her wedding dress.

There was a noise suddenly coming toward them. Heavy boots.

"No, no!" Mamá called. "Don't come in here. Women are dressing!" She bustled over to close the door, but it was too late. Manuel was already there, his hand frozen, raised as if to knock.

María blushed furiously and looked down.

"Manuelito! Out of here! *¡Apúrate!*" Mamá had to push him back, so stunned was he by the sight of María in his wife's wedding dress.

Manuel stumbled outside. Young Blanco, the white hound puppy, loped up to him, all elbows and spit. Manuel squinted in the bright sunlight, absently scratched the dog behind his drooping ears. "Eh, boy." There was a strong smell of petunias and cut grass. Rafaela had planted petunias around their house as well, a large patch of them outside their bedroom window. He smiled. And now, here was María.

He did not love María yet, not as he did his Rafaela, but he was very aware that she regarded him with longing.

"You know what you must do," his father had said. "They are family."

He'd nodded. He was sure one day God would put new love into his heart, for a wife. His only concern was that she must wait for this to happen.

"Eh, Blanco," he said, scratching the dog on his belly now, "the Lord will have to work quickly to resurrect my love." The dog struggled to his feet again and wagged so vigorously his whole body shook. "Yes, yes, He is a God of Resurrections. Doubtless, He knows what He's doing."

Our Hope In You Sustains

BOB pushed the door open with his book, wincing ever so slightly as the noise from the hallway jumbled its way in ahead of him. It made no difference. She didn't move. Still, he tiptoed to her side, holding his breath as though he would awaken a child. Her face was vacant, her eyes staring forward, her mouth caught in a silent O. Her knees were bent under the sheet, probably against bedsores, he thought. "Oh, *Maman*," he whispered.

The room had concrete block walls, painted a creamy white. His grandmother's kitchen curtains hung in the only window – his attempt to make the place seem more like home. But the light wasn't right; it didn't smell like bacon here and there was no sloping wooden floor. BOB fingered the lacy edge of a curtain, remembering when they were new.

"So Les, what do you think?" She'd stepped back, tilting her head this way and that to see how the light filtered through the gauzy white.

"Boy, oh boy, *Maman*! Boy, oh boy!"

She laughed. "Boy, oh boy, indeed!"

"It looks like a fairy tale. Like a movie-star kitchen, *Maman*. Boy, oh boy!"

"Now, let's not pretend this kitchen is a dream come true! I hope the two of us have bigger dreams than that." She'd pulled him to the circle of her arms and ruffled up his hair. He hugged her back. She smelled of roses and fresh bread.

"Aw, *Maman*, you know I'm gonna be a famous writer."

"Like Mr. Maugham and Mr. Hardy and..."

"And Mr. Tolstoy." They'd both laughed at that.

He brought the curtains when she had her last stroke, when he knew she wouldn't be leaving. He didn't have to sneak them in. She was beyond noticing. If she hadn't been, she never would have stood for it. The thought of never going home would have broken her heart.

There was an old photograph of the two of them on the windowsill. BOB picked it up. They were standing outside Forbes Field, people streaming all around. The Pirates won that day. But who had taken the picture? They always went to the games alone – as they did most things. Who among that crowd was kind enough to hesitate for strangers, to pause and snap a picture when his cozy home beckoned? He turned the photo over. On the back was written, *Leslie and Maman share baseball.*

"*Maman*, do you love baseball as much as I do?"

"Well, let's see: the crack of the bat – the wonderful uniforms – sitting in the sunshine watching boys make their dreams come true..." He chewed his lip. "Maybe I'll bring one of the guys next time? From school."

"Sure, honey. Bring anyone you like. Baseball must be shared, eh?" And she'd ruffled his hair like she liked to do.

But he'd never brought a friend. Even at that young age, Leslie Simon treasured what he suspected would be the short time he would have a grandmother, have anyone really, to love just him.

BOB heard her stir. He turned quickly, but she was still again. He shook his head. "Boy, oh boy, *Maman*," he whispered. "I never thought it'd come to this."

He trusted her completely as a child, never wondering about his past until he'd gone to school. One day he came home crying, the questions swirling in his head. What happened to his parents? Was she his mother's mother or his father's mother? Where was his grandfather?

"Leslie, darling, what's the matter?" She'd put her rose scented arms around him, drawn him to her breast. He couldn't speak for a long time, choking on his misery. She finally pushed his head back, brushed the thick black bangs from his forehead and stared into blue eyes that looked at her accusingly.

It had started with his name. Leslie Simon. The other boys at school, and even the girls, couldn't believe he had a girl's name. And a boy's name too, but not in the right order. If he'd been called Simon Leslie, that would have been all right. And then the word he didn't know, that ugly one, soon followed. Bastard. What was that? He knew it had to be bad from the way they sneered it at him, but how? And why? What did it mean?

For the first time, he saw fear in his grand-mother's eyes. Instantly his heart softened. He took a deep breath. "It's my name, *Maman*. They're making fun of Leslie."

"Oh, that!" She laughed now, visibly relieved. "You know, difficult names run in the family! Look at mine – Alexandra. And of course my mother called me Alex. Well," *Maman* chuckled with her memory, "the girls all thought that hilarious! Until one day, I said to them, hey don't blame me if your mother named you something silly, like Edwina or Bernice. Alexander con-quered the world!" She nodded wisely. "That shut them up!"

The next day, after school, when he went to the library to look up the ugly word, his face reddened. He threw his arms over the B pages, afraid someone would see. Then he peeked underneath one arm and read it again. He thought of how his grandmother was so much younger than the other grandmothers; how beautiful and wealthy she looked in the photographs from her youth.

But they were all alone together and always had been poor.

He thought of this and thought of it until an explanation slowly surfaced in his mind. "Boy, oh boy," he whispered in admiration at *Maman*. He wiped his nose on his sleeve and sat up straight. "Okay."

That afternoon he felt the world a different place as he walked home. He was sure some people looked at him kindly, some glanced with a distracted frown, and some passed roughly by, as though he had something that was catching.

The kitchen was full of soupy steam. *Maman* raised her spoon from the pot. "Leslie," she called. "Did you finish your homework at the library?"

He threw his jacket on a chair. "Yes, *Maman*," he answered.

"Come in here." She pointed at him with her spoon. "If I were to ask you what phrase characterizes you, what would you say?"

"What? I don't know what you mean."

"Describe yourself in three words."

"Um..."

"Boy, oh boy! You say it all the time."

"Say what?" he asked.

"Boy, oh boy."

"Oh yeah." He grinned. "I guess."

"So here's what we're gonna do." The spoon went back into the pot. "From now on we're giving you a secret name."

"Like a code?"

"Like a code. We'll use the letters b-o-b."

"But that spells Bob."

She nodded. "Other people may think that, but we'll know that it's BOB – short for Boy, oh boy."

BOB took her cold fingers and gently stroked them. These were the hands that had comforted him, that cooked his meals, that spanked when he was naughty. This nearly empty body once housed the greatest woman he'd ever known. She'd made a home for him, for them, and against all odds, raised him to be a man.

BOB slid to his knees and wrapped his arms around her as far as he was able. "Please, God," he whispered, "please, God, please..." He repeated the words over and over, never finishing his thought, in some bewildered way believing God would understand. Between his pleas he could hear his heart beating and gradually the beat became words, soft and faint, then growing stronger and more insistent. "This will not be her final home. This will not be her final home." A faint scent of roses lingered and he inhaled deeply, comforted.

"Mr. Simon?"

The sound of his name jerked him to his feet. "Yes, ma'am?" BOB was looking at a heavy-set nurse, with bright beady eyes. "Has there been any change since...?"

"Since yesterday? No." She straightened the sheets with a quick pull. "But there's been no decline either." She cocked her head to read the spine of his book. "*War and Peace*?"

He nodded.

"You know she can't..."

"She likes the sound of my voice. Doesn't much matter what it is." He fingered the book. "In the old days, we'd read the classics together. She used to say it was a sin to waste time, and so much of the new stuff was a waste."

"Ah, a lover of the classics! An intellectual!"

His grandmother flinched and BOB caught his breath.

The nurse shook her head, smoothed the bed-covers again. "It doesn't mean anything. Involuntary muscle spasm."

"Oh."

She sized him up, a skinny young man, pale and sad and lonely. Busying herself about the room, she continued briskly, "Are you staying to eat? With her, I mean. You know, just to keep her company..."

"Yes, of course," BOB answered quickly, his eyes on his grandmother. "For her."

The nurse smiled at the floor and as if an afterthought, she took the old lady's pulse, then whisked out of the room, another burst of noise punctuating her exit.

"Well, *Maman*," BOB leaned closer and brushed the hair back from her brow as she used to do for him. "What do you say we eat in tonight? I'm positively starving. And, I've got news. *Maman*, you always said it would happen! I met the girl I'm going to marry. And she's not only beautiful; she's courageous, just like you."

Punctuate Our Ordinary Time

He was six years younger than she and yet in many ways, he seemed much older. She watched him tramp slowly down the hill. He stared at the ground, a sneer gripping his upper lip. Why was he always so unhappy?

"B-O-B!" She loved his name. It was an acronym. He refused to say what it stood for. Brother Of Beelzebub? Boy Orbiting Bees? He said one of those was partly right, which one he wouldn't say. She figured it was "orbiting." That sounded most like him.

"Hello, Trini." BOB looked up when he reached the door, gave her shoulder a squeeze. "Ready?" He could tell she was. She was wearing her new jeans and a shirt he hadn't seen before. Her hair needed combing, but it always looked that way. Something about her efforts to please touched him, made him smile.

"Let me just say goodbye first."

"Of course." He followed her into the house and said hello to her mother while Trini said goodbye. María Elena was nearby, busily teaching the dog a new trick. BOB watched with interest while the old dog snuffled and yawned for a biscuit. María Elena did not cave easily.

"Sit, Cucho, sit up!" She waved a biscuit menacingly. "Up! Up!"

"M-E," he spelled to her, "How old is Cucho?"

"Never mind," she replied, not looking at him. "He can learn."

"I don't think he wants to."

"What's that got to do with it? Do you only do what you feel like doing?"

"Yes."

"Liar."

"María Elena!" Trini stood with her hands on her hips.

"Well, he is. Sometimes." She looked at her sister with an odd expression, one Trini had never seen before.

"Let's get out of here, Trini, before ME lassos us into her school of tricks!" BOB laughed and held open the worn screen door.

They were going to a movie at the Playhouse and, afterwards, dinner at a Lebanese restaurant. Trini hopped into the old Volkswagen. It was just the kind of evening she enjoyed. Finally, a boy, a man, who liked what she liked. It was a thirty-minute drive to the city. Trini put on the radio and settled back, enjoying herself already.

"Mind if I smoke?" BOB pulled out a Marlboro. He lit it before she could answer. She didn't mind, of course. She liked the smell and, besides, she thought it made him look mysterious.

She smiled out the window. "Nice of you to ask."

"What the hell!" BOB slammed on the brakes and stuck out an arm to break Trini's potential crash into the dash.

"Whoa – what – ?"

"Freakin' idiot!" BOB blared his horn three times and pressed hard on the gas as if to make up for lost seconds. "You okay?"

Trini patted her hair. It made no difference. "Of course." She smiled at him but he didn't smile back.

"That idiot could'a killed us; passing on a curve with a double yellow...!"

"Whoa. I said I'm okay."

He stared hard at the road, still frowning.

"Why are you so pissed off?"

"What do you want? Howdy Doody?"

She laughed. "Hardly. But isn't there something between Howdy Doody and deathly miserable?"

"So now I'm deathly miserable?"

Trini sighed. "Never mind." She hesitated. "BOB, I know we haven't been dating that long but I don't get what you're so mad about. I mean, we have a good time when we're together, but I can see it takes you a while to relax, to enjoy yourself. And I can't even imagine what goes on in your head when we're not together."

"So, what do you want to know?" He still stared blankly ahead.

"What makes you happy?"

"You."

She blushed. Too easy. "What else?"

He thought for a minute. "A good movie. A great book. A newspaper article with no grammatical errors. When my socks have no holes. When my burger comes out pink but not bloody." He threw his cigarette butt out the window.

She nodded. "So what makes you mad?"

He raised an eyebrow. "That's harder, Trini." She loved to hear him speak her name. "I have to find a way to make it in the world. To be a man. Have integrity. So, here I am, scraping away, writing, working in a bookstore, letting my grandmother's place go all to hell because I don't know the first thing about taking care of a house. I can hardly even afford to take my girl out."

His girl? "Go on."

He grabbed her hand. "I just don't want to end up like everyone else."

Very gently, she continued, "What's everyone else like?"

"They've all given up – settled! Not me. I'm gonna work like hell to finish my book and when that one's published, I'll write another and another and somehow the truth that people finally recognize will..."

"Will change the world?"

"You're mocking me." He let go her hand.

"No, I don't mean it that way. You don't understand."

He stiffened. "Understand what?"

"You can't change a thing until you become a part of it. And the funny thing is, you already are part of it. You just don't see it yet." She sat back and looked out the window again.

"So, if I'm part of it already, whether or not I see it, I can still change it. The world, I mean."

"Forget the 'aha' and listen to what I'm saying. What's your definition of reality?"

"My definition? What's reality got to do with it?"

"Nothing. Everything." Trini took a deep breath. "You're not really any different from anyone else, but that's okay. You'll find out."

"Find out what?" BOB lit another cigarette.

"You're young."

"You're not so old."

"But I'm not angry anymore. There's this thing about conforming, about obedience, that's actually kind of liberating."

"Oh, sure. That's what all the conformists want you to think. You hear that from Ken?"

"I didn't say being a blockhead is liberating."

"Sorry." He grabbed her hand again. "I should be glad you were dating him. Makes me look good by comparison."

Trini laughed with him. They were coming to the Fortieth Street Bridge now, an old but impressive structure that would carry them across the Allegheny River. The city skyline in the distance looked magical. Like Oz. She cast about for another way to explain.

"BOB, one day you'll realize the incredible beauty of an ordinary life. You'll measure your success by how well you struggled, how you chose to please God, not by the victory itself."

"Oh, so it's God now, is it?" He drew hard on his cigarette and pressed his foot to the gas.

Trini looked out the window at the river. The evening sun danced on the water. "Everything is, eventually, no?"

"You sound like your mother."

She smiled, determined not to take offense. "I once heard a professor say that reality is conformity rooted in agreement with absolute truth. And joy is living in that truth."

They entered Lawrenceville and turned in the direction of Oakland. BOB remained silent. He wouldn't discard information that might be valuable, but he wasn't ready to concede anything yet.

"Conformity doesn't leave much room for ego, does it?"

"Isn't it easier that way?"

"I don't like things easy."

"I know." She watched the traffic light change to red. "Neither do I." They were almost at the theater. "What movie are we seeing?"

"*Purple Rain*."

Trini nodded. "I'd Die For You" was her favorite song.

With Your Guiding Candle

Nunzio woke without stirring. He opened his eyes, pieced together the events of the night before, and smiled. A delicate hand was draped upon his chest. He studied it, squinted and pressed his chin against his neck in an effort to see it more clearly. Thin, brown, devoid of jewelry, long-ish nails, no polish, it could be the hand of a precocious preteen, a new mom with little time to take notice of her appearance, or a teenager, whose grooming waxed and waned with her mood. It looked good against his dark muscled chest.

He could hear the birds sing. It was getting light. In a few minutes, he told himself, he would get up, would have to go. Work would not wait.

"Ooh. Is it morning?" The hand curled shut, ran its way down his belly and slowly uncurled again.

"No." He tried not to laugh, wrapped his hand around hers and pulled it to his lips. "No, Candela."

"Oh, Nunzio, don't be in such a hurry," she whispered with her tongue in his ear. Her slight mahogany form pressed into his. He was hard,

hard all over, as ever, but he peeled her off just the same.

"I have to work. You are nearly too delicious to resist, but I must." This time he raised himself and tossed the covers over her head. Better that she not see him naked. Nunzio was aware of his good looks.

"Hey! What are you..." She fought the blankets, but by the time she emerged he was in the bathroom, in the shower, singing. She laughed, rolled over. Last night had been her triumph. She, Candelaria Vidal, had been saved!

She was leaning against the bar, being pressed into its cold brass railing by two disrespectful boys. The nerve. Was it her fault she was alone? Didn't she get thirsty? She only let them buy her one drink. To what did that entitle them? Surely not what they were thinking! Candelaria had laughed at their jokes, maybe stolen a cigarette so that the skinny one could light it for her... Her eyes were enchanting at close range, after all. But the impertinence – that he, that they should take her kindness as more than she intended – was absurd.

The boys did not see it that way.

And then Nunzio stepped quietly into the tavern. It was his habit to stop for just one, after work. He stood behind the three of them, his reflection in the mirror over the bar silencing them, making them still. After that, it was a simple matter for Nunzio to lay one iron paw on each, and propel them through the door.

Candelaria gasped, "Nunzio!"

"Are you all right, Candelaria?"

She straightened her clothes, tossed her head. "Yes, yes. Thank you. But, you didn't have to..."

"I've a powerful thirst. Let's get out of here." He took her arm and guided her through the door to his truck parked outside.

She didn't ask where they were going. She didn't care. Nunzio Méndez was taking her out.

When they pulled up in front of the William Penn Hotel, Candelaria bit her lip. Here? This was an elegant establishment by any standard – chandeliers, tiny tables with tiny lamps and a big, shiny oaken bar. The plush carpet made walking in high heels difficult. And, Candelaria was hardly dressed for it – Nunzio was still in his work clothes, for goodness sake!

He didn't seem to notice. He smiled at her, then raised an eyebrow to the doormen, who hastily bowed and parted.

This was how, for the first time ever, Candelaria entered a bar on the arm of a man who drew as much attention as she did. She raised her chin. People always looked, but here there were no snickers, no snide remarks about her virtue, no sad old men, eager young boys, lining up to buy her a drink. Nunzio, strong, silent, honorable, was lifting her from the mess she'd made of her reputation, elevating her to the status of "good girl," a woman worthy of selection.

She floated beside him to a seat at the bar. When she was settled he laid one arm along the back of her chair and motioned to the bartender.

"Sir?" The bartender continued polishing a glass. "Something for you and the lady?"

Nunzio locked dark eyes on the man until he looked up. With a clenched jaw he bit his words carefully, daring the bartender to disobey, "Give me an Iron City and the lady will have a champagne cocktail."

The bartender's glass slipped from his hand. "Of course. Right away."

When she was served, Candelaria took a deep breath. "Nunzio?" she whispered, "What are we doing?"

"Having a quiet drink in a nice place."

She looked around, nervous. "I don't think they want us here."

He smiled. "Hungry?"

She nodded.

Nunzio leaned forward slightly and the bartender took a step back. "May I see a menu?"

Candelaria laid her hand on his arm. "For pizza, Nunzio."

He patted her hand. "Never mind. The lady has a taste for pizza tonight."

"What? Still in bed? I can give you a lift home, but you'll have to dress quickly. Here." He threw her a towel.

"Nunzio." She was sitting up now, keeping the covers modestly raised to hide her nakedness. (She could play along.) "Nunzio, why me?"

He kept dressing. "Why not?"

"Well, you're so...um...you know..." She twisted the blanket. "And me, I'm, well..." Candelaria shrugged, then sighed, resigned. "I would appreciate a ride home. Thank you. I'll hurry."

Nunzio only laughed when she conveniently dropped her towel. Quite close to him, she had to bend to retrieve it. He took the opportunity to slap her bottom. "Enough already! *¡Rápido, Candela!*"

Candelaria lived with an elderly aunt. Tía Fermina would scold her for another indiscretion, but she didn't care. This time, it was worth it.

When Nunzio pulled his truck up to the house, Tía Fermina's silhouette could be seen near the window. Nunzio chuckled as the lace curtain fell back into place. "Come on."

To Candelaria's surprise, Nunzio got out of the truck first, opened her door and kept her hand in his, as he walked her to the front stoop. In the bright morning sun, before whoever may be looking (and if Tía Fermina was spying, one could be sure there were neighbors watching as well), Nunzio put his hand under Candelaria's chin and smothered her lips with a kiss. "You were a light last night," he whispered, "a true candle."

She gulped.

He kissed her again. "I work late. Kindly be home when I call." Candelaria's aunt yanked the door open just then. "Ah, Tía Fermina! My apologies for returning your gentle niece at this hour. Please forgive me." Tía Fermina was speechless. Nunzio's huge form blocked the doorway's light as he leaned forward. In confidential tones he confessed, "She is so enchanting, I lost all track of time."

He nodded to a neighbor, as he made his way back to the truck. Nunzio smiled to himself. By noon, it would be all over town.

"Nunzio, what are you doing here?" Carlos walked into the house to find his brother sitting at the dining room table. "I saw your truck in the driveway."

"I was in the neighborhood so I stopped to have lunch with Mamá."

"You children are always welcome!" Mamá laid a plate of bacon and eggs and a basket of tortillas in front of him.

"Thank you, Mamá!" Nunzio rubbed his hands together. "Hot sauce?"

Carlos dropped into the chair next to him. "Carlitos?" Mamá urged, "Eggs? How about a bacon sandwich?"

"Sure, Mamá. Whatever. So, Nunz – you go out last night?"

Nunzio tilted his head, smiled at his plate. He nodded slowly.

"William Penn Hotel?"

His eyes narrowed. "Maybe. What's the difference? A drink is a drink."

"No. A beer is a beer maybe, but a drink at the William Penn Hotel Lounge isn't a drink at Willy's Tavern, eh?"

"I needed a champagne cocktail for a lady." Nunzio chuckled.

"Oh, well. You couldn't get that at Willy's of course. A lady, huh?"

Nunzio's eyes went small again. He curled one hand around his fork and gently touched its tines with the fingertips of his other hand.

Mamá bustled in with a sandwich for Carlos, and the good jar of homemade hot sauce for Nunzio. "Oh, you went out with a girl last night?" She nodded busily. "Good! Good! Anyone we know?"

"I'll say!" Carlos blurted out.

Mamá looked at Nunzio expectantly.

He put down his fork, tore a tortilla in half and slowly scooped it full of egg. "Candelaria. Vidal." He said it firmly without looking at either of them.

Mamá crossed herself and Carlos jumped to his feet.

"That's what I heard. Julio's cousin washes dishes there and he told Julio he saw you two leave together. But I said no way! It couldn't be! Nunzio's picky. He's got standards! And she..."

Nunzio rose too. In his quiet way, he filled the little room with more than his size. "You are right, Carlitos. Miss Vidal meets those standards. Do you or your little friends have anything to say about that?"

Carlos looked helpless.

"Boys! Boys! Sit down. You are grown men. Allow each other room." Mamá shook the jar of hot sauce at them. "*¡Siéntense!*"

Nunzio worked till nine and took a shower before calling Candelaria. "Tía Fermina? How are you? Ah, good, good. May I speak to your niece?" There was a moment of clatter and confusion before he heard Candelaria's voice.

"Nunzio. You're home late."

"I said I would be. I often am. That won't be a problem, will it?"

"What do you mean?"

"I mean I work. I come home and eat and sleep and go back to work again in the morning. On holidays I eat at my mother's. On Fridays I drink too much. Which reminds me, will you go out with me Friday night?"

She laughed. "This is how you ask a girl for a date? No wonder I never see you with anyone!"

"It's true." She couldn't see him shake his head, but she could hear his smile. "Miss Vidal," he cleared his throat, "will you do me the honor of accompanying me on a date this Friday night?"

"Why, it would be my pleasure, Mr. Méndez." She laughed, then suddenly grew quiet. "But, Nunzio...?"

"Yes?"

Very low, "What will they say?"

"Who?"

"People – your family."

Now, he laughed. "They will say it's about time!"

The following Sunday, Carlos and his brother-in-law, Paul, stood in Mamá's kitchen, watching Nunzio shoot baskets at the old hoop next to the barn.

"Well, he definitely looks different," Paul said.

"It just doesn't make any sense!" Carlos insisted. "Nunzio of all people. When he finally

gets around to choosing a girl, he takes that...
that slut?"

Paul stood a little straighter. "Are you sure
she's so bad? I mean, maybe she was wild in
high school or something and..."

"Paul don't you know Candelaria Vidal? People
talk about her all over Pittsburgh – all over the
tri-state area. And Nunzio's such a saint."

Paul's upper lip curled. "Maybe not so much."
He studied his brother-in-law; deliberate, unhur-
ried, sinking every shot. "Could be he's just
being Nunzio."

"What do you mean?"

"Nunzio doesn't mess around. Maybe now
that he's ready for a woman, he wants an
expert."

"You mean a sex-pert."

"Whatever. You know, you almost sound
jealous."

"Ha!"

"Anyway, he probably doesn't want some
young thing he's gonna have to teach and mold.
He wants someone, you know, experienced.
Good."

"Good?"

"Already good, I mean. And she makes him
happy, right?"

"Look at him! But that's beside the point."

"No, my friend. I think that is the point." Paul
remembered the girls he knew before he was
married, the desperate gleam in their eyes, the
hands that would clutch in spite of themselves.
Even his own wife, his Modesta... "You don't
know what makes a girl bad – or what can make

her good. This Candelaria probably needs Nunzio as much as he needs her."

"Hmm," Carlos mused, "sounds like a movie title: What makes them good..."

Three months later, Nunzio sat again at his mother's dining room table. His parents sat with him, his mother with a frown, his father with a quiet, knowing smile.

"But, this is so sudden!"

"Sudden?" Nunzio chuckled, "Mamá, I've waited thirty years. Don't you think I know my own mind?"

Father put his hand over Mamá's. "There is no woman who is good enough for a mother's son. Of course you must make your own choice. We only remind you that there are many people in the world from whom to choose."

"Ah, sí." Nunzio rubbed his chin. "This is the woman for me, though. No other will do."

His father stood. "Then it is settled."

"When she agrees, it will be settled!" Nunzio smiled as he got up to leave.

Father walked with him to the door. He clapped his son on the shoulder with one hand and opened the door with the other. "She will not refuse you. You are doing the right thing by that girl."

Nunzio nodded.

Father stood on the deck, blessing Nunzio as his truck rolled down the long dirt driveway. Then he turned to Mamá. "Are you crying?"

"Yes, I'm crying! Our Nunzio is getting married."

"Isn't that what we wanted?"

"No. It's only what we thought we wanted."

Luminous In Lush And Desert

The Méndez family was a wary tribe, some from modesty, some from pride. They looked with suspicion on those who would dare to become one of them. Just as their brothers had grilled Paul, and to a lesser degree, Claudio (everyone suspecting the Lord himself had guided Claudio to choose their pious daughter), the women intended, each in her own way, to discover what it was about Candelaria that had enchanted their eldest brother, their pillar, their beloved Nunzio. The matter became urgent when he announced Candelaria would become the new Mrs. Méndez as soon as she and her gentle aunt could make the proper arrangements.

"Trinidad, what do you say we take Candelaria out to lunch?" Modesta was at the office. She balanced the phone between her ear and shoulder as she ripped through a stack of mail.
Trini rolled her eyes. "That is the oldest..."
"What?" Modesta interrupted. "Not an ambush, just lunch – a nice friendly lunch – to get

to know her. We'll ask Mamá and María Elena if you want, and we can make it..."

"A family roast?"

"You are so mean sometimes."

"Me? You're the one who wants to scare the poor girl out of her..."

"Poor girl? She's marrying Nunzio!"

Trini was silent. She too was uncomfortable with the thought of Candelaria Vidal marrying her brother, but setting themselves up as obstacles to Nunzio's plan did not seem wise either. "What do you suppose her motive could be? Love?"

Modesta shrugged on her end and nearly dropped the phone. "That or his communion money. Or possibly the thousands of dollars he has saved in jars around his house."

"Oh, Mo."

"Come on! You know he's never spent a cent on anyone. Except Mamá," she hastened to add. Nunzio had bought their mother a new washing machine and a dryer last year. Only he could convince Mamá to give up her beloved wringer washer.

"Did he get the ring?"

"Not yet. You know Nunz. He had to make sure it was a 'yes' before shelling out."

Trini giggled. "I guess we better get this over with before he buys it then."

"That's the spirit!" Modesta said grimly. "We'll meet at the Greek place at one o'clock. I'll phone her."

"Do you know her number?"

"No. But if it's not listed there's a men's room here."

"Oh, dear. I can see how this is going to go..."

"Quit complaining and call María Elena. I'll pick up Mamá myself."

"María Elena is working at the restaurant."

"Perfect. We'll go to Esteban's, then. She won't want to miss the fun!"

"Yeah. The fun."

Candelaria was late. Besides being nervous about the whole thing, she thought it would be better not to be sitting there waiting, a ready target. She dressed as conservatively as someone with a knockout figure could – remembering at the last minute that Modesta was not so named for her dress either. Perhaps Nunzio's mother would be joining them. (The sisters would certainly behave if their mother were there.) Taking comfort in this, she pulled on a straight navy skirt and tucked in her shirt. She left her hair down long. Candelaria's hair was magnificent, chestnut brown and full. She liked the way it felt when the wind lifted it from the collar of her white button-down. Then, fastening a wide leather belt around her waist, as if girding herself for battle, she found her purse and went to bid her aunt goodbye.

"Now," Tía Fermina fussed, "You look lovely in that skirt and blouse. Why don't you always dress that way?"

"Goodbye, *mi Tía*. Wish me luck!"

"Luck? I thought you were having a luncheon? What does luck have to do with eating lunch?"

Esteban's was busy, noisy in a friendly way.

"Over here, Candelaria! Over here!" Modesta half stood to get her future sister-in-law's attention.

"Just go over there and get her!" Trini muttered.

"No can do, Sweetie, but don't let me stop you." Modesta gave Trini a glittering imitation smile.

María Elena saw Candelaria hesitating by the door. "This way, Candelaria. Wow. You look great."

"Thank you," Candelaria smiled with more gratitude than the simple compliment warranted. "Hello, girls," she said when they reached the table. "It was so nice of you to invite me."

"Please," María Elena started, but Modesta broke in.

"Oh, don't mention it," she gushed. "We were just dying to get to know you better. I mean, we couldn't imagine the magic you must have worked on our brother. After all, Nunzio is very particular when it comes to...well, everything." Trini and María Elena stared at her. "What?" Modesta demanded.

"Of course he is," Candelaria agreed. "Believe me, no one was more surprised than I when he asked me out." She laughed. "When he more or less just took me out."

"Oh," Modesta simpered, "so that's not the way you usually do it? I mean, is there a protocol or...?"

"Modesta!" Trini scolded.

María Elena coughed. "Drinks, anyone?"

"I'll have a white wine. In fact, can I see the wine list?" Modesta answered briskly.

Candelaria sat back. "I'll just have an iced tea, please."

"Touché," María Elena murmured, not looking at anyone in particular.

"Well, Trini, I guess it's just you and me!"

Trini took the wine list from Modesta and gave it back to María Elena. "We won't be needing this. Better bring us two Bloody Marys." When María Elena left, Trini said to Modesta, "Now quit it, Mo, before you get us in trouble! Remember, María Elena has to work here."

Candelaria refrained from giggling. She cleared her throat instead. "Will your mother be joining us?"

Modesta inspected her water glass. "Oh, she had some thing she had to do or something. I called her, but you know Mamá and answering machines. She just hates technology."

"Ah, yes. I heard the washing machine story," Candelaria answered with a smile.

"Now, Candelaria, you live with your aunt, right?"

"Yes. With Tía Fermina."

"Isn't that cozy," Modesta said. "You must save a bundle living with the old dear. No rent, no utilities.

"Actually," Candelaria said softly, "I pay rent and I pay her utilities. We pretend to share the costs for food and such. The only thing she really pays for is her taxes. Would you like to see my bank statements, or will my word do?"

"Really." Modesta put her hand to her throat. "You don't have to get your back up. I was only making conversation..."

"Candelaria, you'll have to excuse my sister," María Elena was back with the drinks. "This actually is her way of making conversation. Don't take it personally."

"It's true," Trini sighed. "She's a jerk to everyone."

"I'm right here," Modesta said.

Trini ignored her. "You sure you still want in?"

Candelaria looked down and nodded, a secret smile on her lips.

"You guys better order," María Elena said. "I mean, I know you're family and all, but Teb will be wondering why I'm not shoveling food over here."

"Teb?" said Candelaria.

"The owner," María Elena explained. "How about the Teb Salad? It's good today – not too garlicky..."

They ordered salads all around and María Elena hurried off. Candelaria sat watching her hosts, one so simple and natural, the other a polished replica of the beauty she was trying to preserve. It crossed her mind that Modesta was very unhappy and *why*, she wondered, *after what looked like years of trying, did the wealth she accumulated not assuage her pain?*

"Oh," Trinidad said casually, "I spoke to Claudio this morning."

"Yes?" The breathlessness Modesta attached to that one word was unmistakable to the female heart. In an instant, Candelaria knew the source of Modesta's pain.

Trini took a big gulp of her drink and coughed. "Yes. He can't bring Mercedes to Mamá's next Saturday. She's going to a birthday party."

"Oh."

"So you don't have to tutor her."

"Oh."

Candelaria kept her eyes on her iced tea.

Against her better judgment, Modesta asked softly, "Did he say anything else?"

Trini shook her head. "Hey, you guys ever hear of a band called Encuentro? BOB is suddenly into them. He heard them on that public radio station he listens to."

So they talked about music for a while. Candelaria asked about the curious name of BOB and they speculated wildly on what it could stand for. Then María Elena returned with their salads, relieved that everyone was finally getting along.

It wasn't until the end of the meal, till Trini was in the ladies room and María Elena nowhere in sight, that Modesta and Candelaria finally resorted to honesty. Modesta was staring hard at her guest, weighing which would be best to attack first, Candelaria's advanced age, her inexpensive attire, or perhaps the makeup that she obviously purchased at a discount drug store.

Candelaria sat poised on the edge of her chair.

"You may have fooled my soft-hearted brother, but you don't fool me." Modesta threw the gauntlet down, discarding the obvious and going straight for the throat.

"Your brother is no fool," Candelaria parried. "You mistake his stoicism for a lack of imagination, or worse, for inexperience!"

"Ah! If experience is to be the great leveler..."

"Then you and I are equals, are we not?"

Modesta gasped. "How dare you!"

"Modesta, don't make an enemy of me because I had the strength to do what you could not."

"What I..." Modesta sputtered, "and what exactly is that?"

Candelaria took a last sip of her tea, just melted ice cubes now, and pressed the napkin to her lips before replying, "I waited."

The weight of those two words dealt a lethal blow. Modesta's mind reeled. How could Candelaria know her secret? Had she told Nunzio? She didn't remember confiding in him. Did he tell his betrothed? Could Trini have told Nunzio? "Excuse me," she muttered, hurrying to join Trini in the restroom.

Candelaria pressed her face with the back of her hand, then she placed one finger against her upper lip. She touched beads of sweat. When she looked up again, a man was approaching the table where Candelaria now sat alone.

She automatically sized him up: wedding ring, tall, handsome, perhaps a little weak around the chin. She smiled, wondering who he was.

"How do you do," the gentleman bowed, which soothed her hurt pride. "I'm Paul Martin, Modesta's husband."

She gave him her hand. "Candelaria Vidal."

He nodded, though he felt like whistling. "Modesta just went to the ladies room. You can wait here if you like."

"What's wrong?" His eyes were kind, his voice gentle.

"I don't know," she almost laughed. "Maybe you should let go of my hand before the girls return?"

"Oh." He let go. "Sorry."

"No, no, I'm teasing you." She pushed out a chair for him. "So tell me, Paul, how do I get them to accept me?"

"Ha! Couldn't tell you. Maybe have a child?" When she looked down, he quickly sat. "I'm sorry. That was rude." Candelaria looked away. Paul gazed over her head. The bathroom door was inscrutable. "Hey, don't let them upset you. If it's any consolation they did it to me too."

"They did?"

"Yep. The brothers too."

"Really. So I should expect a visit from you and Carlos?"

"Right," he laughed. "And don't forget Claudio."

"Oh, yeah. Was he grilled too?"

"Well, it was different with him. You know, they were all kind of in awe of Adela. When she agreed to marry Claudio, I think they saw the hand of God. And then of course, they knew him. He dated Modesta, once upon a time!" Paul chuckled, but Candelaria heard bitterness.

"And it doesn't bother you?"

"What?"

"That your wife's ex is in the family?"

"No." Paul looked at Modesta's plate. He used a breadstick to draw an arrow in the dressing that was puddled there. "I trust Claudio."

Candelaria wished she had a cigarette. She murmured, "And Modesta?"

"I love Modesta." He looked up at Candelaria with an air of longing that made her blush. "You've never been married before, have you?"

She shook her head.

"Okay." He glanced toward the ladies room once more; there was still no sign of movement. "Here's the thing. In the beginning it's all honeymoon – like when you fell in love. She is the thing that makes your sun rise in the morning and set in glory every night. You can't believe God was good enough to make such a person just for you! And then, bit by bit, it changes. She picks a fight, gets in a mood. She snaps at you, maybe abuses a waitress. She claims she doesn't like puppies, won't let you get a dog. She doesn't iron or cook or do the wash. To keep peace you keep house. And when you fight, you always apologize first. You try to make her happy. And sometimes it works. Occasionally you see a glimmer of the girl she used to be. But even that grows rare. The weeks turn into months, the months to years and then one day you can no longer tell if you're happy or just resigned." He leaned in closer. "And that's when you know you're there."

"Where?"

"In the desert."

"The desert?" she whispered.

He nodded. "Ever hear of saints who live in ecstasy of the Godhead? And then one day they lose it, and are thrown into deep despair? It's like a cold wind, or a wall, or a desert."

"You mean like the wall that runners hit?"

"Kind of."

"And saints...," Candelaria frowned. "Didn't Mother Teresa speak of it?"

"Yes." Paul put down the breadstick. "Well, married people endure it too. Things become routine. The novelty wears off." Candelaria thought about this. She was no virgin, and the wonder of a good man choosing her to be his wife was so new to her, she felt certain it would never end. She wanted to ask if this must happen to everyone; she wanted to be absolutely sure, but she only said, "And how long does it take for this to happen?"

"Ah, how long. Now that's a question! For some, ten years, for some fifteen." He glanced at the closed bathroom door. "Less time for others."

"But why...?"

"And the thing is, there will always be others. You don't stop being attracted to other people, nor do they to you. It's not malicious; it's just human nature. Each has his own allure."

Candelaria looked at Paul with new eyes. She naturally assumed Modesta was sought after, but perhaps Paul had been tempted too. And he had reason to give in, if such an opportunity occurred. "And when this happens, if it happens, what keeps one married? What keeps you in it?"

"Hope." He smiled. "A woman wants a knight in shining armor, someone to sweep her off her feet. In her heart, I guess she never stops wanting this. So, if I stand by her, if I never give up, perhaps one day she'll look at me that way. Again."

"That's the secret?"

He nodded. "Never give up. If you want your marriage to succeed, don't run from the desert. Nunzio never does anything lightly. He'll stand by you forever. When it gets tiresome, remember that."

Modesta and Trini were suddenly back, rifling through their purses, counting out money. "Remember what?" Modesta asked, not even looking at her husband. "And where did you come from? He's not boring you, is he, Candelaria?"

"Oh, no. On the contrary." Candelaria pushed her chair back and stood up. It was the first time she'd met someone who wasn't on the lookout for somebody better. Well, the second time, if she counted Nunzio.

Relentless Miracle

Nunzio stood on the porch, rolling his head from shoulder to shoulder until the crackling in his neck ceased. Then he clasped his hands behind his back, two mitts joined together and lifted with all his strength, making his spine snap, hard. He could not see Mr. Cruz, cowering behind him.

"Ah, Mr. Méndez! What do you think of the house? She's a beauty, *sí?*"

Nunzio turned slowly and let his eyes wander over the peeling paint, the dirty windows, past Mr. Cruz's head to where his Candelaria was pushing faded curtains aside. She was studying the view from various vantage points, obviously delighted with this, the very first house they had considered buying. "A beauty, eh?" He chuckled.

"Well, well then, Nunzio. May I call you Nunzio? It's about time you settled down and made a home for yourself! Your mother would..."

"My mother?" Nunzio looked startled. "Candelaria!"

She turned and smiled at him. "Yes, Nunzio?"

"Candela, do you think Mamá would like the house?"

"This one?" She sauntered over to the screen door, which separated the living room from a wide wooden porch. "Well. It's not very clean."

"*Sí, sí*." Nunzio laughed. "Tía Fermina would like it better!"

"Nunzio! Don't make fun of my poor aunt!" But she laughed too.

Mr. Cruz joined in their laughter, hesitantly. He cleared his throat. "Of course the place hasn't been lived in for some time and the former owner was old, well older, when he passed. Tsk, tsk." He shook his balding head.

"Who was the former owner?" Candelaria asked.

"Ah, a kind man. A sad man. "

"Did he live alone?"

"For the last ten years. His only daughter married and left about that time. She was, let's see, he was forty-six when she was born. Twenty-two, yes, she was twenty-two and he was sixty-eight. Seventy-eight when he passed. Poor Enrique!"

Nunzio looked up. "Enrique Ruiz?"

"Ah, *sí*. The same."

"Old man Ruiz."

"Oh, but he was not always that way. I was only ten years old when he married the prettiest girl in the *barrio*!"

"There's a *barrio* here? In Pittsburgh?"

Mr. Cruz chuckled. "Well, no. Not exactly. It's what we called the neighborhood, back then. To remind us."

"Oh." Candelaria smiled. "Was it a big wedding?"

"Ah, *sí* Everyone was there! A pig and a lamb. Roasted on spits. A cake as big as a room and *empanadas*. Oh, the *empanadas*! And the dancing! Enrique and Margarita could dance like Fred and Ginger. The girls were spellbound and the men all jealous. Even I, even a ten-year-old boy could tell it was the wedding of royalty!"

"Wow." Candelaria looked dreamy.

"Yes, wow. But the story didn't end the way it began..."

Enrique and Margarita were in love. They'd been in love since high school. When Margarita dropped out to help at home, Enrique came to her house and studied with her after school.

"Enrique! What are you doing here?" Margarita asked when he appeared at her door.

"We're going to learn together." He dropped a stack of books on her kitchen table. "What shall we talk about if I know more than you do?"

"Enrique, don't be silly. You will never know more than I!" She sat next to him and obediently opened a book. "Books do not contain all knowledge," she murmured.

His arm went round her as they studied.

They looked for one another at church on Sunday and sang the familiar hymns together under the watchful eyes of parents and maiden aunts. Enrique cut her family's lawn; Margarita presented jars of canned tomatoes to his mother. When graduation time came, Enrique gave Margarita flowers to wear to the ceremony. She cried with happiness to see him in his cap and gown.

And afterward, he did not go to the steel mill like the other boys. He had no interest in the local restaurant where Mexican food was making something of a stir. He was not inclined to join the military, even if they would have paid for his education. Enrique was smart, but he was concerned for those less fortunate. He wanted to become a teacher.

He enrolled at the teacher's college in the next town over. It was an hour-and-a-half drive each way, and it cost more than he and his family had, combined; pure insanity to everyone but Margarita. She told him, "Go. You may not know more than me, but you can learn more than your friends, your classmates and certainly, their children. You can lead them to a better way."

With her encouragement and four bank loans he was able to achieve it. The day after he graduated college, Enrique took Margarita with him to accept a starting job at the local Junior High School. "I will get them when they're young and steer them in the right direction, before they become discouraged!"

"You will please God."

"I'd rather please you."

She laughed. They stood near the flagpole, watching two young men lower the American flag, carefully folding it so that no corner touched the ground. "You will be their hero, as you are mine," Margarita whispered to him.

"As you are mine," he answered. Then turning toward her, he took something from his pocket. "Margarita, will you stand by me forever? Will you be my wife?" He slipped the ring on her finger before she could reply.

Margarita nearly fainted. It was as if all her hopes and dreams were coming true with his. "Yes, yes! Oh, yes, my love!"

Enrique squeezed her hand, reluctant to do more in case a student should see.

"And then they had that magnificent wedding and lived happily ever after, right?" Candelaria held up a small silver *milagro* in the shape of a girl's face. "I found this on the windowsill."

"Ah, that was hers! You would think so, eh? They were happy, so happy for a time. But, life isn't always as we wish, is it? Margarita longed for a child more than anything."

Candelaria paled. Nunzio steadfastly looked away. They had been trying to conceive since they were married; she had secretly been trying since they met. Neither one had considered that it might not happen.

Candelaria might have missed her period last week. She kept this to herself, fearing it was just late and she would be disappointed once again. She frowned at the *milagro*. "But you said they had a daughter..."

Margarita watched her husband coming up the sidewalk. He was handsome, fit and well into his forties. She still teased him about the crushes of seventh grade girls. He swung into their front gate.

"Rita! Darling!" Enrique threw down his jacket and grabbed her by the waist. "What smells so good? I'm starving!"

She laughed. "You're always starving!"

He held her at arm's length for a moment. "If I am it is only because you are such a good wife!"

She blushed.

After supper, as she washed the dishes and Enrique corrected papers on the dining room table, Margarita told herself it was a good life, a wonderful life, really. She had no right to be dissatisfied. Certainly if Enrique could bear the lack of children, she could do no less. If her period was late again, it was no cause for jubilation. She had gotten both their hopes up before, to no avail.

But this time was different. This time her period did not come. With mounting joy and disbelief she waited until a month had passed before saying anything. Enrique went with her to the doctor's office.

"Well, you two! Better late than never, eh?" Dr. Santiago sat them both in his office. He adjusted his glasses and peered at Margarita. "My dear, I know you've suffered disappointments before, so my advice is to relax. Perhaps cut down on coffee and cigarettes and strenuous activity. We shall see. Who can predict what God has planned?"

Enrique and Margarita held tightly to each other's hands. It took great effort for them to keep from shouting with gladness.

For six months they prayed and planned. They painted the back bedroom for a nursery and accepted a gift, a crib from a neighbor's attic. Margarita happily put on weight. Enrique brought home melons and pickles, ice cream and peanut butter, in case a craving should strike.

One morning, Margarita came downstairs wearing a new necklace. Enrique was just about to leave for school and he lifted the silver medals on her chain.

"Saint Gerard," she quickly said.

"The patron saint of expectant mothers?"

"Yes." She nodded, smiled.

"And the other? A *milagro*?" He kissed her cheek, amused that she would place a traditional good luck charm next to a holy relic.

"Just in case. It was my mother's. And besides, I've always liked *milagros*."

"Of course, my love." Enrique smiled. He fingered it, then frowned. "This is in the shape of a girl's face, not a baby's." Margarita shivered. "What if we have a boy?"

"It was my mother's," she repeated.

"Of course, Love. It's perfect."

That night at supper, Enrique watched his wife. She moved with grace about the table; pregnancy became her. Her silver medals glinted in the candlelight. St. Gerard and a *milagro*. He wondered at the *milagro*'s shape. A baby would have been more appropriate. Why a girl? Perhaps the mother? A tiny pin of fear pricked him.

Later, when they lay in bed, reading side by side, he heard Margarita's breathing, deep and regular. Her book was lying next to her. He shut off the lamp she faced, and after switching off his own, slipped from the bed. He was on his knees for a long time, while Margarita pretended to sleep.

The days grew long. They sat on their front porch. It was cooler outside than in. "Enrique?"

"Yes, Rita dear?"

"Remember all the times I cried? Before? In our first years?"

He nodded.

"And you always said to trust in God. That all would come out right?"

"I do."

She leaned against him, placed his hand upon her belly. "You were right, my love."

"And you," he answered. "You were right as well."

"When?"

"When you said all knowledge does not come from books."

With her other hand, she touched the *milagro*, but he did not see.

And then the trouble started. Margarita began bleeding. A bit at first, then more, then less, but constantly. She moaned, "Enrique, why? Will the baby be all right?"

"Hush, now Rita. We are in good hands."

But the doctor shook his head. He took Enrique aside and told him, "I can save one or the other, but not both. It's complicated I'm afraid. You'll have to choose."

Enrique stammered, "Choose? How much time do I, do we have?"

Dr. Santiago blanched. He assumed the choice was simple. A man must have his wife! What was this need of time? "A day or two at most. The sooner we address this, the better. Then she can get on with her life."

Her life, her life. The words echoed in Enrique's head. He bowed and led the doctor to the door.

"Enrique." It was a whisper, but he heard it.

"Sleep, Rita. Don't disturb yourself." He steeled himself, held back the tears.

Her face was calm, her eyes wide with understanding. "You know what we must do."

"I know you must sleep now. You need your rest to heal."

She smiled at him. "I cannot heal."

"My Rita!" He knelt by the bed. She took his head upon her breast and stroked the graying hair.

In the morning, when Dr. Santiago arrived, Enrique met him at the door. He motioned for the doctor to take a seat on the porch swing.

"How is our patient this morning?" Dr. Santiago asked.

"Margarita is resting now. We were awake most of the night."

The doctor frowned. "Was that wise? Given her condition I would have thought..."

"I don't know whether it was wise," Enrique said. "But it was necessary."

The doctor stood. "If she is resting I will come back later. I can do it here, but I'd rather perform the termination at the clinic."

"The what?"

"The termination. We will remove the fetus and make repairs to stop the bleeding. She will most likely be barren as a result, but this is a small price to pay for her life, eh?"

"No." Enrique shook his head slowly, as though it weighed upon his shoulders.

"No?"

"There will be no 'termination.' You may not sacrifice our child."

"Have some sense, Enrique! I cannot save them both. I told you. It is your wife or your child."

"I know, I know."

"You are assigning her to death!"

"What must you do to save the child?"

The doctor stood with open mouth. "I...you...I...!" He sputtered, taking off his glasses, shifting his weight from one foot to the other, putting the glasses back on.

"Must she go to the clinic or can she stay with me?"

"I will return," he answered. And with that he left, his lingering look of incredulity etched in Enrique's mind.

"So he was mad," Nunzio said. He uncrossed his arms and leaned on the rail. The rings for the porch swing were still attached to the ceiling above him.

"Poor thing," Candelaria murmured.

"Ah, *sí*," Mr. Cruz nodded. For a moment he looked like a bobble head, but then his eyes softened. "He hired me to cut his grass. I trimmed the bushes, swept the walk, tried to keep things tidy. For her. Her bed was by the window. She'd look out sometimes and smile. She always wore her necklace, with the St. Gerard and the *milagro.* "

"How long did she live?" asked Candelaria.

"Until the babe was born. She never left her bed, of course. Enrique went to school each day. He came home and cooked their supper, did their wash. He played her favorite albums on the old record player. I knew they dreamed of their wedding dance. I dreamed of it myself."

"How could he live with himself after that?" Nunzio asked brusquely.

"I do not say it was easy. He was himself only when he was with his daughter, a beautiful girl, just like her mother. At other times he was quiet, much too quiet. People thought him bitter. They soon called him 'Old Man Ruiz.'"

"Well, I think it's sweet and noble. Sometimes the right choice is the harder one." Candelaria put her hands on her hips and surveyed the house and yard.

"Your wife is wise," said Mr. Cruz. "You will never know more than she does, you know."

"Ha!" was all Nunzio said, but he did not disagree.

That night Candelaria told Nunzio she wanted the house. She rubbed her thumb back and forth, massaging the *milagro* in her pocket. "It will be an honor to take care of it. The way Margarita would have wanted."

"Oh! Mr. Cruz got to you with that story! A house is just a house."

"No, Nunzio. A house is not just a house and a marriage is not just a marriage and a child is not just a child!" She raised her eyebrows at this last part and he dropped the paper he was reading.

"Candela! My love, are you telling me...?"

She nodded furiously.

He scooped her up and swung her high in his strong arms. "My love, my love! It's true?"

Hours later when Candelaria stirred in her sleep, Nunzio pulled the sheets up to her chin, gently, gently, so as not to wake her. It was an easy reach, from where he knelt.

Mr. Cruz had the contract ready. The young Méndez couple was coming to sign for the house. When they arrived, Candelaria was wearing the silver *milagro* on a chain around her neck. Mr. Cruz' eyes were sharp. He took her hands. "Congratulations, my dear!"

Candelaria blushed. "Thank you."

Nunzio interrupted, "Are you always so enthusiastic when you sell a house?"

"Ah, *sí* The house! A double blessing!"

They signed the papers nervously and Nunzio went to the basement to check on something. Candelaria turned to Mr. Cruz. "So Enrique Ruiz chose his child." She tilted her head to one side and fingered her necklace. "How did he finally make the choice?"

Mr. Cruz nodded toward the window where Margarita's bed had stood. "He did not make the choice. She did."

Margarita shook her husband. "It's time, my love."

He was instantly awake. "You mean...?" He clutched her in the sheets, very warm and moist now with anticipation.

"It's going to be all right," she soothed. "You'll learn to do without me. The child will have a good strong father; a smart man who can lead her..."

"No!" he cried. "I will not do it. I cannot choose your death!"

"You must," she reminded him. "I do not wish to live in place of our child. That would be a kind of hell to me." Enrique raised his eyes to hers. "You would do me no favor, choosing me." She'd never seen him cry before. "You have always been a hero, to your students, to your family and to me. A true hero does the hard thing even when no one understands."

"If you loved me you would not ask this of me," he choked.

"But, Darling, I don't ask it. God does." She took the chain from around her neck, pressed it into his hand. "Only make me this one promise: raise her a good Catholic. And tell her I loved her from the first, and I always shall."

"And the baby?" Candelaria asked. "How did she turn out?"

Mr. Cruz smiled at his feet. "Raising a child is a curious thing. He named her Consuela."

"Consolation," Candelaria murmured.

"*Sí*. You are acquainted with names and their meanings?"

Candelaria only blushed.

"They say 'the Lord giveth and the Lord taketh away.' He knew she was to be his consolation, but he did not know she would be much more." Mr. Cruz rubbed the back of his neck. "The Good Lord took away Enrique's wife and in her place, gave him a savior. You see, Enrique was heart-broken; he lost his faith when his poor wife died. But he never forgot his promise to her. He had the baby baptized and when it was time for her to go to school, he sent her to St. Luke's. There she made her first Confession, first Communion, Confirmation. And being a teacher, he studied with her; being her father, he celebrated all her sacraments. He confessed to me that her innocent faith saved him. He came back to the Church because of Consuela. He was even considering becoming a deacon when she moved to Chicago."

"Chicago?"

"Ah, *sí*. She is married now, to a doctor. She came back to be with her father when he died. You know, she looks so much like Margarita, she thought he mistook her at the end. Just before he died he said, 'I've missed you for so long! I lay awake at night, wondering... but you were certain, you were so sure.' Then he took her hand in his, and kissed it.

"She said his last words were curious. She had to lean in close to hear. He murmured softly, oh so softly, 'I was a good teacher, but a slow learner...it took me a whole lifetime...Love...to learn...what you always knew...'"

Grace Cup To The Dying

María walked barefoot in the furrowed road. She didn't mind the hot sun or sharp stones in her path as she hurried along. She was on her way to her cousin's house. Encarnación was engaged to marry Manuel's brother.

"María! What took you so long?" Encarnación opened the door herself and drew her cousin inside.

"Oh," María smiled, embarrassed. "You have more important things on your mind. Please don't trouble yourself about me."

Encarnación laughed. "Oziel just phoned me! Can you believe it? He said he cannot go for more than a few hours without hearing the sound of my voice."

"He did?" María's heart squeezed painfully. She had neither telephone nor any lover who would say such things to her. Mamá said the telephone was a prideful thing – a sure sin. If the Lord had meant us to be constantly chattering to one another, so important that we must not miss one word at any time from anyone, he would have made us birds. Her father always laughed at that and said Encarnación would have made a lovely chicken, indeed. But María thought of Rafaela, and how she would have been a pure white dove, or maybe a graceful swan.

She coughed.

"Are you all right? Here, sit down. You walked all the way, didn't you?" Happiness made Encarnación generous. Didn't she have everything a girl could wish for? Her Oziel would one day take over his family's ranch. He had told her so, himself. And he was handsome and strong and devoted to her. Poor María was older than she, and had no prospects at all. How sad, Encarnación clucked to herself, that Oziel's brother did not ask for her hand in marriage! She shook her head.

"You must take better care of yourself." She smoothed María's hair and tucked a curl back into her low bun. "There, that's better." Encarnación twirled around. "How do like my new dress? I'm not supposed to wear it yet. I put it on just to show you. It's part of my trousseau."

"But," María faltered, "I thought we were to sew your clothes. Look, I brought my needles and scissors." She pulled a cloth bag from her pocket. She had come to her cousin's for the express purpose of preparing her trousseau.

Encarnación waved airily. "No, need! Mamá finally agreed to let me buy everything I required – two more dresses and a beautiful little suit for the trip and, of course, (here she lowered her voice considerably) new undergarments and a new nightgown." She giggled.

"You don't have to show me those." María forced a laugh as well. She wanted to be happy for her cousin, but her head hurt and she felt dizzy. She slipped the modest sewing bag back into her pocket. "May I have a drink of water?"

"Oh, the tea! I forgot the tea. And lemon and sugar." Encarnación bustled away and María laid her head upon her arms. She nearly cried.

With all her heart she wished her cousin well, but she was keenly aware that she, María, was only getting older, and that Manuel should have asked her to marry him by now, if that was his intention. "But it must not be. No. It isn't," she whispered to herself. Just in time, she raised her head again.

"Here we are." Encarnación sailed back into the room, poured the tea and added lemon and sugar, as she knew María liked. "This will perk you up. You're probably not getting enough rest at night. Does Manuel call on you after work? I never see him anymore. Except at church, of course."

"Of course." María smiled thinly and took a sip of tea. It was strong and aromatic. She lifted her chin. "Manuel," she coughed again, "Manuel is getting a teaching certificate. He works hard at his studies and still finds time to help his family with the ranch. I'm not surprised you never see him."

"Ah, but surely you do? And teaching? That's wonderful. Now he'll have an occupation." Encarnación added the thought, *so that his brother can have the ranch*, but aloud she said, "So that he can raise a family. Very important!

Tell me, when he's completed his training will he be at the grammar school or will he teach the higher grades?"

María kept her eyes on her cup of tea. "Neither. He hopes to teach at the mission school."

María started coughing again and for a long while, she couldn't stop. By the time she did, she was too exhausted to continue her visit so she excused herself and began the long walk home.

"When did it start?" a voice asked briskly.

"Yesterday." Mamá spoke slowly and distinctly, a little loudly into the telephone. "Just before lunch."

"Is that all? If she gets worse call the doctor back tomorrow. One day of flu isn't going to kill anyone."

"But...," Mamá gasped, not used to such a tone.

"Tomorrow."

Mamá heard the phone click and she handed the receiver to Encarnación.

"Tía Flaca, I'm sure she'll be all right. Come back and borrow the phone any time," Encarnación said hurriedly. "And don't worry. It isn't like what Raph...I mean, María is very strong."

"Ah, *sí*," María's mama answered absently and quickly left.

María was in bed for three weeks and still no better. By the time the doctor came, listened to her chest and took her temperature, her illness was advanced. "Why do you people always wait to call me?" he muttered in self-defense.

Mamá gave María sips of water, cold cloths when the fever burned, warm blankets for chills. María moaned softly, trying to hide her pain. There seemed a knife blade in her back, her side, her back again. She couldn't get comfortable lying down, yet she lacked the strength to sit. Mamá sat by the bed with her rosary at night, when her work was done.

María also prayed silently for her recovery. She did not care for herself, her life had become a burden with the unanswered question of Manuel's love, but she did not want to leave this earth and make her parents bereft again. They were still mourning Rafaela, after all.

Manuel appeared frequently, nervously turning his hat in his hand. "Mamá Flaca," he called her by the name he'd used when he was married to her other daughter, "How is María today?"

"Ah," Mamá Flaca always raised her hands to heaven. "Better today, I think." But he was not fooled.

Each day he entered the sickroom and sat next to the bed. At first María was overjoyed that he thought enough of her to come. But when day followed day, and week followed week, and still he did not mention the future, didn't urge her to get well for his sake, she began to lose heart. If he loved her, if he cared for her at all, surely he would have asked by now. Slowly, as she descended into the misery of fever and pain, the sickness blended with her heartache, until the two were one.

Manuel sat next to her bed on this day, his elbows on his knees, hands turning, turning the brim of his black hat while lines of worry creased his forehead.

María mustered a weak smile.

He reached over and touched her hand. It was burning. "I will fetch your mother," he said, getting up to do so.

She shook her head. "Please, don't go," she whispered.

He sat again. "Very well. Shall I tell you what happened in school yesterday?"

She nodded.

"Well, you know I'm working with the fourth grade class. We're studying the first chapter of the Bible, Genesis and creation, and one rough boy, his name is Gabriel..."

"Like the angel," she murmured, and coughed again.

"Ah, *sí*. Well, he asked me if God really made the world in six days and rested on the seventh. I said, *Sí*. Then he asked me what God did when He rested!" Manuel smiled, shook his head. "And I said, what do you do when you rest, Gabriel? And he said, I beat up my brother." He laughed, and María tried to also, but her laugh was choked and soon the coughing took over. She couldn't stop.

Manuel ran to get her mother, who came in with a steaming basin and a cloth. "Out, out!" she shooed him away.

He stood in the kitchen, shifting from one foot to the other, not sure what to do.

When Mamá Flaca returned with the basin and cloth, he saw bloodstains.

"Why do you come here?" she muttered.

"Because I...," he hesitated, "because I care about María. She stayed with Rafaela until she died."

"And this is how you repay her kindness? Will you watch her die as well?"

"I...she..."

"How are the studies going, Manuel?" María's father was standing in the doorway. He looked from Mamá to Manuel and then made his way to the kitchen sink. He began washing his hands.

"Fine, fine," Manuel answered, head bowed.

"You will make a good teacher," Mamá Flaca said, picking up a broom with more energy than necessary. "It is a good living. And the high school is closed all summer, so you will have plenty of time to work the ranch. You will have two incomes. More than enough to raise a family. We had nothing when we started out."

"Nothing but each other," Papá nodded, drying his hands now with a small rough cloth.

Manuel blushed. "I will pray for María," he answered, bowing low and backing toward the door and the hot day outside.

Manuel walked miserably, so lost in thought that he didn't notice the scorched path and the hard stones protruding underfoot. "Beloved," he prayed, "How am I to answer this? I am happy enough without a wife, though happiness is not my aim. When my Rafaela died I had to wait a suitable time, and then I waited longer,

just to make certain that I was not still in love
with her memory. I prayed to love María, to be
sure, and now, watching her suffer, so patient
and uncomplaining, I never saw her so noble,
so grown up. She wears suffering more beautifully than any woman dressed in jewels and
finery. I am not even worthy of her." He walked
on, squinting at the sun. "You know. You made
her. Oh, dear God, if You take her home now,
think of what it will do to her family! She is all
they have."

I am all they have.

"Ah, *sí, sí.*" Manuel knelt under a tree beside
the road that led back to the mission school.
He put one hand on the spindly trunk and with
the other, crossed himself. "You are all." He hesitated, considering something carefully. Finally,
he took a deep breath, "Beloved, I make this
humble request – me, the least of all your creatures. I have grown to love this woman, so much
so that if You will spare her life, restore her, then
I shall dedicate myself to You. All the days of my
life are Yours, Beloved, whatever they number
on this earth."

Manuel stayed like that; the sun sinking lower
and lower beneath the horizon. He prayed and
prayed as if his life depended upon it. As if hers
did, as well.

Wisdom To The Living

María Elena's father glanced up from his book as she entered. "What? Alone tonight?" he asked, looking over his glasses at a girl who was turning into a woman before his eyes.

"Yes, Dad." She dropped onto the sofa next to him. "You didn't like Charlie very much anyway, did you?"

He returned to his book. "I thought him a perfectly nice boy."

"You did?" She stood again.

"María Elena!" her mother called. "You missed supper. Come get something to eat."

"You'd better go see Mamá. What kept you at school so long?"

"Oh, another paper."

"What was this one about?"

"The Civil War."

Her father shook his head. "History will wait. Your mother won't."

In the kitchen María Elena's mother was taking a dish of tortillas from the oven. "These will be all dried out now."

"Don't be silly, Mamá. I'll eat them. I'm not Carlos."

"He's the one who told me I should warm them for you when you're late."

María Elena laughed. "The things he thinks are important!"

Her mother smiled too. "Why are you so late?"

"It's just school, Mother."

"You know, both Carlos and Trini ate at home tonight." She looked proud. María Elena knew Mamá loved to be surrounded by her children. She wanted them to still want her. She gave her mother a hug. "Now, now – you'll make me drop these!"

They sat at the dining room table, her mother watching María Elena pick at her food. "Where is Charlie tonight?"

"Oh, he had to go to his mom's. She's like you. She likes to feed people."

"There's nothing wrong with taking care of family, María Elena."

"I know." She dipped a piece of tortilla into her gravy.

"Are you no longer seeing this one, either?"

"School keeps me really busy. I finally decided to major next year in both history and poly sci." Her mother looked quizzical. "Political Science."

"Oh." She nodded.

"And it's not like we were...we weren't seeing each other that long or anything."

Her mother kept nodding.

"I mean, well, you know."

"No, my dear, I really don't."

María Elena sighed. "It's not like you and dad or something."

"Ah."

They were silent as María Elena pretended to eat.

"You know," her mother said finally, "your father was not perfect when I met him."

María Elena kept her eyes on her plate. "I'm not looking for perfect."

"Whatever happened to that other one? Stephen?"

María Elena snorted. "He wasn't right for me."

"You liked him well enough to bring him for Christmas. We gave him a pair of socks and a box of cookies. It's none of my business, of course, but one day he's in our prayers and the next day..." she snapped her fingers. "Just like that, he's gone!"

"Mamá, I liked him, but he had this habit. I wasn't sure and when I asked Dad what he thought, he said something like, 'Well, I couldn't live with it.' And really Mamá, neither could I."

"What did he do that was so bad?"

"Every day after work he stopped at a bar."

"Oh."

"Oh? What?" María Elena made little swirls in her gravy.

"What did Stephen do for a living?'

"He was a stock broker, a commodities broker, you know, he traded other peoples' money all day."

"That sounds difficult."

"I'll say."

"So he had to unwind after work each day?"

"Well, yes, I guess."

Her mother nodded. "And your father didn't like this."

María Elena raised her eyes to her mother's. "I didn't like it."

"And Charlie. What does he do that you do not like?"

María Elena thought for a moment, as if she couldn't remember. "He doesn't see the future."

Her mother was smiling at her now.

"Mom, it's not funny."

"No, no. Of course not. When did you notice this?"

"After Dad..." She stuffed her tortilla into her mouth.

"When?"

"Never mind," she mumbled with her mouth full.

Her mother reached over and placed her hand on top of her youngest daughter's. María Elena was perpetual joy to her. Smart, head-strong, with her father's height and her mother's thick black hair, she didn't know yet how beautiful she was. Mamá had watched María Elena's sisters and brothers grow to adults and now here was her last, blossoming, flailing about with her judgments and decrees. "María Elena," the name was like a song to her still, "did you ask your father what he thought of Charlie?"

She nodded.

"Well, and what did he say?"

"He said Charlie didn't know where he was. He didn't know where he wanted to be five years from now, ten years from now. And then he said, that was fine and all, but he couldn't live with it."

Her mother was still smiling. "And he couldn't live with Stephen, either?"

"Not if he had to go to a bar every night after work."

Her mother just frowned. She closed her hand over her daughter's and gave it a squeeze.

"You might as well tell me," María Elena sighed.

"Love, if one has to unwind after a hard day at work, it's not a sin. If you didn't like him going to a bar you could have encouraged another way. Nunzio goes to the gym – or he did until Candelaria got him those weights for the basement. Paul golfs. Carlos goes to a bar and drinks Coke."

María Elena fixed her gaze suddenly upon her mother's face. "What did Dad do?"

"He went to a bar."

"What?"

"Of course, for him it was always to talk to the parent of a troubled student or to solve a crisis with the Puerto Ricans at Cut Flower, but it was always after work and it always took place in a bar."

"What did you do?"

"I cooked supper and waited. And what about your Charlie?"

"But, Mamá, if he has no vision..."

"María Elena, do you mean to tell me that you do know where you will be and what you will be doing ten years from now?" María Elena stood. She took her plate to the sink and began rinsing it. Her mother followed with the tortilla basket.

"No one knows what the future holds, Dear. Not you, not Charlie," she got a far away look in her eyes, "and certainly not your father!"

María Elena turned to her mother, exasperation filling her face. "Did I do wrong, Mamá?"

"*Querida*, you did what you did. Whether it was right or wrong is not for me to say. What I don't understand is why you are seeking your father's approval."

María Elena shrugged. "He's my father. And he's wise."

"Yes, well, there's wisdom and then there is wisdom." She placed her hands on María Elena's shoulders. "Your father married me. Do you really want a man who reminds you of your mother?" María Elena laughed. Smiling, Mamá began drying the clean dishes. She examined the chipped handle of a cup. "Did you know your father thought he would be a priest at one time?"

"What? Dad?"

Mamá nodded.

"What happened?"

"It wasn't meant to be. Your father wished to thank the Lord for answering his prayers and in his enthusiasm, he chose a path that the Lord did not mean for him. You see dear, the future that your father imagined was not God's will. We can't always know or even plan what we should be doing in ten years time because it isn't up to us. Our job is to determine the will of our Lord now and do that to the best of our abilities."

"Dad, a priest? I just don't see it."

"Yes, well, had he been, you wouldn't be here to see it, eh?"

María Elena considered this. "Mamá," she said, a little hushed, "none of us would be here."

Her mother nodded, wiping the last cup and saucer and setting them in the cupboard. "God is truly wise. When you need approval, seek it there."

May We Be Made Worthy

"Okay," María Elena said, sitting up and rubbing her eyes. "What are you doing?"

"Nothing. Go back to sleep." Trini tried to hide the calendar she was marking.

"Weren't you on a date?"

Trini nodded, hunched over, writing by the glow of a flashlight.

"What time is it?"

"Please shut up and go back to sleep!"

María Elena flounced back under the covers. Soon she could be heard snoring blissfully. Trini frowned and put away her scribbling. "It can't be," she muttered. "Two years already?" She peeled off her clothes, put on an old T-shirt that used to belong to Nunzio and slipped into bed. The moon lit up the small bedroom. She watched the shadow of a tree branch move on the wall, but it wasn't the light that was keeping her awake. She couldn't stop thinking about BOB.

By the time they had met, Trini was a ripe fruit, warm and luscious. BOB could feel the heat of her desire, but he did not ask this thing of her and he even withdrew when she was ready to suggest it. At first she found this amusing.

Trini didn't need a hot embrace; no moist, fragrant encounter to feel loved. BOB held her hand. He lit her cigarette and showed great tact, instinctively understanding that she never smoked in front of her family. With her he discussed ideas, philosophies, even God. She sensed that he respected her, admired her, was thankful when she waited for him to open the door, allowed him to pull out her chair.

Had so much time gone by so soon? Trini got up on an elbow, clicked the flashlight on the calendar again. Yes. It had been two amazing, astonishing years.

The next afternoon BOB took Trini for a walk in the woods behind her house. They crunched through fallen leaves. "Can you believe summer's nearly over?" Trini said.

"Takes me by surprise every year," he replied, nodding.

Trini laughed. "That's not what I mean! Do you know where you were, exactly two years ago, today?"

BOB was looking at the ground. A slow smile came to his lips. "I believe I was being bullied into *Glorious Pursuit*," he murmured. "Little did I know..."

She gave him a playful shove. "And is it? Glorious, I mean?"

He stopped her in the leaves, gently brushed her hair back. "*Glorious* barely scrapes the surface of its splendor."

"Oh," she whispered. "Then you would still have come? If you'd known?"

"Of course, Trini. Only sooner. I think I would have run." He looked at her as if seeing for the first time her lips, her eyes, her forehead. His gaze returned to her lips, full and round, inclined to chap when winter came but now so soft, so soft. Her mouth drew his. It pressed and gnawed till he could hardly breathe. His grasp tightened. This time he could not stop.

Afterwards she watched his face. He disentangled a leaf from her hair, the hair that had entangled him a short while before. His eyes were stormy, so serious. She waited, but he didn't speak. He helped her to her feet.

They walked a bit. "BOB?" Trini squeezed his hand.

He kept his gazed fixed straight ahead, but returned the pressure. "I couldn't help myself." He lowered his head, smiled at the ground and softly added, "My Love."

They did not make love again.

Trini shrugged. She told herself it didn't matter. BOB loved her, she was sure. But in time the doubts crept in. What if she didn't please him? What if she had been no good?

Or worse, what if she had been too good? Oh, no.

"Bless me father, for I have sinned. It's been nearly a year since my last confession," Trini knelt in the dark, believing this was a good place to start.

"Ah. Continue, my child."

She had come to St. Anthony's Church, preferring a priest she didn't know, or more accurately, one who didn't know her. "Father, I need to confess a sin of, well, of acquiescence."

"To what did you acquiesce?"

"To love."

He chuckled or cleared his throat, she wasn't sure which.

"I know we're supposed to wait, but I didn't. And then I discovered the person whom I thought I was in love with wasn't, you know, the one, and by the time I met the right person he didn't want to do it, and I think I made him do it and now I may have ruined everything..." She swallowed hard to keep from crying.

"My child, it is hurtful to our Lord when we sin, but when we draw others into sin, well, that is more painful than anything."

"I know. I mean, I'm sure. I didn't mean to hurt him, to disrespect him or myself, but I thought at the time...at the time I thought I was being, you know, generous. I mean, don't all men want that and really, what's the big deal?"

"Why don't you tell me what the big deal is?"

"What?"

"If it's no big deal, why are you here? Why are you afraid it's ruined everything?"

"Oh." Trini sat back on her heels. She wasn't used to discussing her sins like this. Usually confession was more like a recitation, a laundry list of mistakes she'd made. But this sin was not that. She knelt upright again. "This time was different," she whispered. "It was a big deal this time."

"And you sound surprised."

She nodded, forgetting he could not see her assent.

"Child, the Lord created sex as a beautiful gift to married couples. You are not married?"

"No."

"Well, in this world it's hard to understand the nature of sex and love unless you educate yourself. Doubtless your good parents did their best, but a former generation often takes for granted the understanding they possess. Sex is not like candy, to be shared with whoever asks or looks hungry. You do no favor to a man by sleeping with him. In fact, you do him a greater favor by keeping him chaste."

"Oh."

"Yes. It sounds to me as though your love interest understands this."

"Oh."

"For your penance I'm going to ask you to say the Rosary, concentrating particularly on the Sorrowful Mysteries, and the ways in which our sin crucified the Lord. You understand, you will not commit this sin again. By confessing it to be sin, you know better now."

"Yes, Father. No one ever explained it to me like that before."

"See if you can't find a small book called *The Knowledge Of The Holy* by A.W. Tozer. It will help you realize the majesty of God, the perfect love He bears us. It will help you understand."

She nodded again.

"Now recite your Act Of Contrition, and I'll give you absolution."

She let his prayers wash over her, feeling for the first time as though her confession meant something; as though it made a difference. When he was finished, he blessed her and added one more thing before she left the confessional. "You have God's forgiveness. Now you must ask pardon of the one you love."

BOB's manner toward Trini hadn't changed. He called her, took her out. They saw the new Meryl Streep film. Afterwards, they dined at their favorite restaurant. His left hand was lying close enough for her to touch, his right gestured earnestly as he spoke about the message behind *Sophie's Choice*. He talked on and on. Trini finally lost it.

"BOB!"

"Yes? What is it?"

"I, I don't know how to say this."

"You don't believe our choices define our lives?"

"No – yes! I mean, I'm not talking about the movie." *But*, she thought, *of all the times to consider choices...* "BOB, I've been wanting to ask you about that day, you know, when we took that walk." She hesitated, longing to say more, but fearing his response. "First of all," she took a deep breath, "I'm so sorry."

He blinked. "Trini, it wasn't your fault. I should have...I couldn't..." He looked at her helplessly, then continued more solemnly, "I should be begging your pardon."

She shook her head. "And that's not all. I have to know, are you...am I... too, too...?"

"Too?"

She took a deep breath. In a hushed voice she asked, "BOB, do you think I'm a tramp?"

He tried hard, but failed not to laugh. "I think you're a weirdo. What kind of question is that?"

"Well, I was thinking...we only...we made love that one time and never again. So either I'm very bad at it, or I'm too, you know, too good," she finally blurted out. "And I know I'm not that bad, so..."

"Trini," his words dropped like marbles from a cliff, "How is it that you know your standing, if one were to rank such a skill?"

She cleared her throat. "I'm not a child, BOB. I've been told a thing or two, and let's face it, I'm older than you. I've had relationships before, that is, I'm no...well..."

"You are an experienced woman." She was relieved to hear laughter in his voice. He grabbed her hand. "But you're also a child! Did you think I expected or even cared whether you were a virgin?"

"Sort of."

They were silent as a waitress set a large dish of rice on their table. She placed a basket of flat bread and various meats around it. When she walked away again, Trini almost spoke, but BOB very deliberately took both her hands in his. "Okay, listen. Here's the thing. Do you agree that grace builds on nature?"

She frowned. "Are we back to the movie?"

"No. This is still us. Do you agree?"

She blanked at first, then answered, "Yeah, I guess."

"Then isn't it your nature that I love? And your nature is composed of everything, all the things you've done, everything you know and those things you're willing to learn." He leaned across the table and drew her to him and into a kiss. Then he sat back, grinning.

She touched her face with the back of her hand. "So, you forgive me then?"

He nodded. "If God forgives us, how can we do less?"

"How do you know God forgives us?"

"I asked Him to. Didn't you?" He scooped some rice with a piece of bread and handed it to her.

She thought, *how does he know me that well?* "You know we can't do it again," she whispered, keeping her eyes on the bread and rice.

He nodded again. "I know. With great wealth, my Love, comes great responsibility. Your knowledge; my restraint."

"Wow."

They ate, BOB turning over a question in his mind, Trini asking one. "So, when?"

"When we are man and wife, of course."

Trini dropped her bread.

Of Your Infinite Clemency

María Elena leaned her head on her hand and sighed. She wondered whether it was too early to sneak a little house wine into a coffee mug?

"Hey, Sunshine, here comes a new table. Look alive!"

Too early *and* too late. The bartender jerked his chiseled chin toward a new group of customers, hesitating just inside the door.

María Elena resisted the urge to stick out her tongue. She turned and stretched a smile across her face instead. "Welcome to Esteban's!" She glanced up at two women in fur coats, she couldn't see how many were behind them... "Table for...four?" she guessed.

"Three." A slender blond man with a rugged chin that matched the bartender's, staggered from behind the women. He caught his breath and tried not to notice María Elena trying not to notice the braces on his legs, his two canes, the cuffs of which reached nearly to his elbows.

"Danilo! I didn't see you there, behind your lovely friends." The women softened. Suddenly they looked almost friendly. "Hey, Teb," María Elena turned to the bartender, but he had mysteriously disappeared. She shrugged. "How about a window?" Slowly, but with no backward glance, María Elena led them to a table by a window and pulled out the chair she would have chosen for herself. The women quickly took Danilo's arms and tried to make him sit.

He laughed to cover his embarrassment. "Okay, okay, ladies. Don't break the merchandise!" He studied María Elena's face and then as if suddenly remembering why he was there, he said, "Could you bring us some water right away María Elena? And ask my brother to make me a scotch, rocks. Girls?"

"Oh, Campari and soda, I guess." The blonde one was struggling to pull off her coat. María Elena eased her out and draped the coat neatly on a chair.

"Man, you're good." Danilo's eyes devoured María Elena.

"And I'll have a spritzer." A brunette with impossibly shiny hair sank into the chair across from Danilo. She reached out to touch his hand. "You were right, Sweetie, the decor *is* very New York."

"See, Peaches? I told you you'd like it. And this is only the beginning..."

María Elena smiled, returned to the bar and scooped ice for their water.

The bartender returned. "And for the *ménage*?"

"Teb, you're a creep. Scotch rocks, of course. Campari and soda for the blonde and..."

"A spritzer?"

"How'd you guess?"

"It's a gift."

María Elena popped a lemon twist into her mouth and added one to the glass, while Teb poured. He nodded. "So my little bro's on a double date?

"Your imagination is only surpassed by your enormous..."

"Don't say it!"

"Ego!"

"And don't take a year. Here comes another crowd."

"Thanks, Sherlock. Be right back." She hurried to the table and set the drinks down with a smile. "Your waiter will be by in a minute." One of the women's chairs was empty. She turned to Danilo. "Lose one already, Nilo?"

He blushed and looked down, but she saw he was smiling. "I just told Peaches to get a good look at my brother. Don't want to hog all the wealth," he said.

María Elena laughed and welcomed the next group waiting to be seated.

Danilo and his friends took a long time to order and even longer to eat. They lingered over dessert, then after-dinner drinks and finally, when the other customers and a lot of the staff had gone home, Danilo struggled to his feet. He staggered to the bar and leaned there, waiting for Teb to notice him.

It didn't take long. Teb was backing into the bar area with a case of champagne. "Yeah, I know," he called to someone in the kitchen, "but it's the best wine for the price and as long as you drink it after the Asti..." He turned suddenly and when he saw Nilo he immediately looked down. The bottles clanged a little as he put them away.

"You gotta be more careful with the good stuff," Nilo said, leaning over the bar to watch.

"How would you know?" Teb returned, sullenly.

"Oh, I know." He leaned over a little farther and in a loud whisper he said, "I remember!"

Teb straightened suddenly. "You allowed to drink that much?" he demanded.

"Nope." Nilo grinned.

"Well, this is the last time." And Teb turned to his register.

"What do you care, *Esteban*? It's not like I'm *driving*." And Nilo went into gales of laughter.

Teb didn't turn around. He glared at the checks in his hand. "Dinner's on me," he muttered.

"Why, thank you, Bro!" Nilo nearly shouted.

María Elena came hurrying over. "Hey, Nilo. Need something?"

Danilo swayed in his braces. "I need...I need." He looked dreamily at María Elena. "Never mind," he said softly. "I never been much good at figuring out what I need." He looked at Teb's back. "Ha! Right, Teb? Right? You agree? Ha!" Suddenly he slumped and he would have sunk to the floor if María Elena hadn't been there to catch him.

"Hey, Teb!"

Instantly, Teb was on his other side, propping him up. "Hey, you little idiot," his voice softened, "Not you, María Elena."

"Ha." She was watching Nilo's girlfriends approach.

"What's going on?" the blonde one said.

The brunette frowned. "Is he okay?"

"Peaches?" María Elena said, "How much did he drink?"

"He'll be all right," Teb said. "You ladies have a car?"

"Well, yeah, but..."

"Go on home, then. We'll take care of him."

"Oh." They looked relieved. "Well, thanks," Peaches said.

The blonde made a show of kissing Danilo on his passed-out head before wiggling into her furs and following her girlfriend out the door.

"He knows better," Teb said angrily, laying his brother in a chair. "Where's his coat?"

"I don't think he had one," María Elena looked around. "I remember thinking how nice he looked in that jacket..."

"Yeah, real nice," Teb muttered. "It'll look great covered in puke. I'll call you..."

"Teb!"

He straightened up. "Well, what do you want from me? It's embarrassing. He's a mess. Look at him!"

Nilo was laying with his hair in his eyes, his shirt half unbuttoned, showing a thin, hairless chest. His wide mouth was slack, his whole body limp with the release that only comes from total unconsciousness.

María Elena was thinking of a time when he was young and vibrant and the world stretched in front of him, ready to be conquered.

"Hey, watch this one!" Danilo had yelled from the diving board.

"Nilo! Be careful," she had laughed.

"Jackknife!" He'd stretched and bent his body so that it cut the water with barely a ripple.

"That's nothing!" Teb had countered. "Do you dare to take on *El Toro*?" He'd put his fingers up for horns and snorted, pawing the ground with one bare foot and then whoosh! He'd sprung into action, twisting and turning like a corkscrew into the water.

María Elena had clapped and laughed. She was only sixteen; she would always be sixteen and they would stay young forever...

The accident happened the following year. Afterwards, she was only able to picture Nilo as he was at seventeen, and now, as a young man of twenty-one. The four years in between were gone, disappeared. Those were the years in hospitals, in therapy, in more hospitals and in court. Endless battles for strength and for money. Well, they got the money, anyway. That's what Nilo always said with a forced gaiety, one nonchalant hand in the air.

"Nilo! Nilo wake up. You're dreaming." Teb was leaning over his little brother. He'd tucked him into his own bed while he stretched out on the couch. Danilo's cry awakened him.

Nilo struggled to sit up. "I...can't...I can't..."

"You're okay. You're at my place."

Nilo blinked. He rubbed his head. "How'd I...?"

"I brought you here. You know, it doesn't impress a girl when you pass out on a date. Especially when you're still at the restaurant."

"Oh."

"You're covered with sweat. Here." Teb found a towel and threw it to him. "What were you dreaming about?"

"Same as always," Nilo murmured. "*El Toro.*"

Danilo and his women friends came in again the following week. The women called him Nilo after they'd heard María Elena, and he called them Peaches and Cream. María Elena took the trouble to be nicer to his friends this time. "Spritzer, Peaches?"

"Why, yes. Thank you." She laid her hand on Danilo's arm. "Have you change for a pack of Camels?"

He frowned. "I thought...you quit."

"I did, I did, Dear, but now I have one of my awful headaches and I think a few puffs will put me right."

Danilo and Cream rummaged for change. Nilo finally came up with a five-dollar bill. "María Elena, can I trouble you for change?"

"For Camels? Of course. I'll be right back." She took the five and returned minutes later with their change and a small plate holding the open pack of cigarettes and matches with the Esteban logo.

"Oh, how lovely!" Peaches said in an exaggerated voice.

"If that doesn't work," María Elena leaned in confidentially, "Teb over there swears by snake bite." Peaches looked puzzled. "For headache. Never heard of it?" Peaches shook her head. "Double shot of Yukon Jack with a tiny layer of Rose's Lime Juice on top." María Elena winked and Danilo burst into a laugh. He lit Peaches' cigarette to soothe her hurt feelings.

"What kind of name is that, anyway?" Peaches pouted.

"'Teb? Nickname. Peaches." María Elena swallowed her laughter and the gentleman in question gave a wink from his post behind the bar. Peaches tossed her hair over her shoulder, arching her back a bit in the process.

Later, Cream and Peaches were arguing about something when María Elena caught Danilo watching her.

"What gives with the *ménage*?" Teb gave a nod toward their table.

"You know, you're a jerk. One day you're gonna get in trouble saying stuff like that!" María Elena scolded.

"Hey, maybe *Nilo* could be your date!"

"What?"

"For your sister's wedding. Got a date yet?"

"You...are a jerk."

"Yeah, you already said..."

The following week Teb's brother returned, escorting the lovely Peaches wearing a very tight pink suit. After their meal, she wiggled to the restroom and Nilo casually leaned back in his chair, pretending to scrutinize the bill. He said to María Elena, "So, who does my dashing brother take around these days?"

"To tell you the truth, I don't think he's seeing anyone."

"Really? In this business?"

"This business takes up all his time."

"What do you think of Miss Pink Suit?"

"Peaches?"

"Yeah. I thought he'd go for her."

"You really want your brother to go out with someone?"

He looked down, played with his knife. "You know why he doesn't."

She frowned.

"'Cause of me."

"What? That's crazy," she laughed.

"Is it?" His eyes turned on her with such a longing that she blushed. "You know. It's all my fault."

"Hey, he's an adult. He can decide whom to date. And when."

Nilo shook his head. "He's a baby and you know it." Danilo suddenly looked older, wiser. "If we hadn't been competing, I never would have done it. But it was my choice, not his. And now his life is ruined."

María Elena's eyes grew bigger. Danilo was a cripple and cocky robust Esteban was the one whose life was ruined? "What in the world do you mean?" she asked.

"You remember *El Toro*?"

"You mean that stupid dive Teb used to do?"

"Yeah." Nilo looked down. "We made it into a contest. Like a dare. *El Toro* was doing anything you thought you couldn't do; you were afraid to do. That last car chase? That was my *El Toro*."

María Elena froze.

The sounds of the restaurant came to her from far away. She was standing in a field, the summer she turned seventeen. There was a full moon and kids all around. Someone said, "He can't do it. Get Teb. He's the crazy one. He's the man. Get Teb."

But nobody got Teb. Nilo slid behind the wheel. The other boy swayed as he threw himself into his car and revved the engine. María Elena heard Nilo yell, "*El Toro!*" and they took off. The next sound she heard was a sickening crash – metal on metal. There was no screaming until she reached the site. Then the screams wouldn't stop...

Maria Elena tapped her chin. Poor Nilo looked so hopeful... "Maybe I can help," she finally said.

Teb called, "Hey, you on a break or something?"

María Elena returned to the bar. "Teb?"

He nodded toward the mezzanine. "Can you help Pamela clear station three? There's a party of twelve coming in."

"Yeah, sure." She watched Teb watching Peaches wiggle from the pay phone to the ladies room. "Interested?"

He whistled under his breath. "Nah. Don't think so."

"Why don't you quit thinking and just give it a shot?"

He stiffened. "Thought about it. Maybe if she was with someone besides my brother. But that," he jerked his head toward Danilo, "would be taking candy from a baby."

"You've never stolen a girl from another man?"

Teb laughed at the bottles he was counting. "Hey, I don't steal from brothers. Or from crips."

She winced. "You'd be doing him a favor," she said softly.

He raised an eyebrow. "Him or you?"

María Elena pulled out her book and carefully checked her drink orders. "You know I love Nilo. We've always been friends." She snapped her book shut. "And how can I help wanting what he wants, especially when it's for someone else's good?"

Teb didn't answer, but when she returned from the mezzanine, Peaches was perched at the bar, her head perilously close to Teb's. María Elena chuckled as she went by.

"But it was so discouraging! I mean, look at me." Peaches hopped off her barstool and spun on her toes. Teb whistled again. "I wooed him for months, and he was absolutely no closer to popping the question."

Teb laughed, a little too loudly. "Well, there's your answer then! Who told you *you* were supposed to do the wooing?"

"Oh, please!"

"And you know we only want what we can't have."

"But he's a..." She clapped her hand over her mouth just in time. "He's a man."

"He's a man. Rules of the game, Kitten."

"There are no more rules. This is the Eighties for God's sake!"

"Yeah. How's that working for you?" Teb put a glass of wine in front of her. "Now take this back to your table or your very disinterested boyfriend's gonna dump your wooing ass."

"Hey, he's not my boyfriend!" But she took the glass and sipped it as she wiggled and swayed back to her seat.

A little later Peaches walked Danilo to the door. He raised his hand in a goodbye to María Elena, with a look she mistook for gratitude.

Late the following night Trini came in to give María Elena a ride home. One or two tables remained, romantic couples, old and young. An overly-dressed, overly-made-up woman sat at the bar, sipping a whiskey sour, her weary eyes fixed on Teb. At the other end of the bar a scruffy carpenter-type stared vacantly.

"Trini!" Teb threw his bar rag over his shoulder and grinned. "What brings you into our humble establishment?"

Trini jerked her chin toward the table that María Elena was just clearing. A customer was lingering at the table. He must have said something funny because María Elena suddenly threw her head back and Trini smiled at her sister's bubbling laughter.

"Oh, I can give her a lift," Teb said quickly. He grabbed a wine glass and set it down before Trini.

"No, thanks." Trini laughed and turned her glass upside down. "To both."

Teb shrugged and ducked into the kitchen. A sigh drew Trini's attention to the carpenter, who was now on the edge of his stool, eyes wide. She heard him say quietly, "You know that girl?"

"She's my sister," Trini answered.

He didn't move at all, but whispered, "And he's the luckiest guy in the world..."

Trini blanched. She leaned forward a little and yes, it *was* he. Teb's little brother was getting up from the table with María Elena's help. Lucky? The lights shone on his metal braces.

"Who is he?" The carpenter asked.

"The owner's brother."

"You know what happened there?"

"He got creamed in a car accident. The other driver was drunk. Law suit..."

"No! She's a gold digger then?"

"No!" Trini coughed. "No way. They're just friends. They went to school together. Anyway, he gave his brother all the money so he could buy this place. You know, Esteban?"

The carpenter shook his head. Apparently he didn't understand because he said again, "Lucky bastard."

The made-up lady must have thought this funny because she burst into a laugh.

Discovering Holy Treasure

Fine weather and celebration do not always coincide, but an engagement is worthy of celebration in any weather. The party was reminiscent of the day they met – another family picnic. Of course, this time it was family and soon to be family, but BOB was already considered family anyway. And since the weather refused to cooperate, the picnic was held indoors.

Modesta circled the buffet. Her *empanadas* (yes – she had to go to all the trouble of making *empanadas* to celebrate her sister's happiness!) were going quickly. "Mamá, where are the rest of the *empanadas*?"

Mamá bustled in. "Dear, dear, are they gone already? We'll have to put out the rest of the chicken salad rolls." She removed the plate, rearranged a few dishes and left again, pushing her hair back.

Modesta wandered out to the enclosed porch. The men were there, drinking, smoking, clapping BOB on the back as if they were welcoming him into a secret club. With difficulty, Modesta refrained from rolling her eyes. She sidled up to BOB and took a cigarette from his pocket.

He raised his eyebrows. "Help yourself. Sis."

"Not so fast, Mister. You and Trini aren't hitched yet!"

Emboldened by his new status, he grinned at her. "Sure we are." He lit her cigarette. "I didn't know you smoked."

"I don't." She cocked her head to one side and took a long, slow drag. Modesta knew how to work a cigarette, a room, a man.

Paul came up behind her. "Very effective, but how 'bout you let him in the family before scaring him off?"

BOB laughed and sauntered toward the kitchen while Modesta watched, perplexity marring her perfect come-hither look. When she turned back to her husband he had disappeared too, and Claudio stood in his place. Modesta caught her breath. Her heart beat faster.

He shook his head. "Smoking makes you look so sad."

She put out the cigarette and changed the subject. "How do you like my dress?" Modesta ran her hands down its very straight skirt and swayed her hips a little.

Claudio frowned. "It's beautiful. Is it new?"

She smiled at her shoes. "Yes. You always liked me in blue."

"You mean, I used to. Years ago."

"No, I mean now. I was thinking of you when I tried it on."

"Oh, Mo." Claudio gave a whistle and looked away. He saw Nunzio and his father-in-law, watching them. "So! What about this happy news?" He nodded toward the kitchen. "Were you surprised?"

Modesta's smile faded. "You could have knocked me over with a feather," she admitted. "Of course, it breaks my heart a little, every time, but this one really got to me. Claudio..."

He gripped her elbow, hard. "Mo. Trini deserves to be happy and if that boy can make her so, then good for them. Remember when you were engaged?"

She winced.

"I remember my party like it was yesterday. Adela was radiant. Your parents were so proud."

Each word was another wound. "Yes, well, Paul and I didn't make them proud, remember?"

"You mean because you two ran off? Adela thought it was very romantic. I bet your mom and Trini did, too."

"Romantic?" Modesta laughed a mirthless laugh. "Did she think we were in love?"

"Of course! What else?"

Other words came to Modesta's mind: desperate – jealous – envious and full of hate. She tossed her head. "It doesn't matter now."

"Mo?" Claudio looked at her closely. "It does matter now. Now more than ever."

"Modesta! Come and show us that dance step you and Paul did last Christmas. Was it hard to learn? BOB is hopeless when it comes to dancing!" Trini burst through the door and grabbed her sister's hand. "You don't mind, Claudio, do you?"

"No, no. Please!" He laughed at her excited face, a face that looked so eagerly to what lay ahead.

Modesta managed to stay within Claudio's line of vision for the rest of the party, but she didn't dare speak to him again. She didn't want to hear him shatter her hope, her last lingering hope that he might still care for her a little. She danced with Paul, helped Mamá to serve, said only glowing things about her sister and future brother-in-law, but it was all an act. A play for an audience of one, she told herself, a show for Claudio.

Finally, just when her enthusiasm was flagging, when she knew she could take no more, it was over. Paul stood on the driveway smoking with Nunzio and BOB. Claudio led a very sleepy Mercedes to the car, where she promptly laid down in the back seat and began to snore. The men were still speaking of such things as politics and sports when Claudio slipped away to thank Mamá and take his leave. He saw Modesta by the door, standing in a pool of porch light, breathtaking and alone. He gave her a quick wave.

"Claudio, wait. Tell me, what did you mean?"

"When?"

"When you said it matters now more than ever."

He took both of her hands. They were smooth and soft, but cold. "You're missing out, Mo, and of all things that could be called sad, that is the saddest."

"No, Claudio, no. What I'm missing is true love. And that's the saddest thing of all!" Her eyes beseeched him to understand.

He led her to the porch railing and sat with her on its edge. "Mo, there's love all around you! If you pine for a love that isn't yours, you miss the love you have. Look at your family. They adore you! At work, they can't do without you for a day. Your husband does his best to fulfill your every desire. My own Mercedes worships you!"

Modesta swallowed, tried not to ask, but she couldn't help it. "And you, Claudio?" she whispered.

"You are a good friend and a dear sister to me, Mo." She turned away. "Modesta, please understand, I didn't marry Adela because you broke my heart. I married her because she mended it. She was rare and strong and beautiful."

"Oh, on the inside – I know, I know! Like I could never be!"

"On the inside and on the outside, Mo. When she woke in the morning – she'd get up and start the coffee and brush her hair. She had so much hair! And climb back into bed to wake me." He looked down. "She never complained. You know, I worried that I didn't make enough money. And she wanted lots of children. But she never worried. She said, 'God knows best' and she meant it. My life was a poem, because of her."

Modesta was quiet.

"Paul loves you like that."

"But Claudio, he isn't..."

Claudio stopped her with a look. "If I have to remind you every time I see you, this will get monotonous. Stop taking him for granted, Modesta. Love is love, no matter where it comes from."

She smiled wearily and kissed his cheek. "Good night, Claudio. Tell Mercedes I'll help her with her math on Saturday. When I'm finished at the office."

The following days were flat and lifeless for Modesta. Paul appeared not to notice her melancholy. He kept up a constant barrage of corny jokes and dinners out. By Saturday morning, when yellow roses arrived at her office, when they were carried to her desk and filled the room with a delicious fragrance, Modesta could feel her pulse quicken. Could they be? No! Yellow roses were Paul's favorite...but he would never do such a thing, would he? She turned the vase around. In all their years together, he had only sent her flowers twice. His surprise was always jewelry, "something lasting," he would say. Yes, yes, she was sure, she was positive they were, they must be from Claudio.

She sat in front of the tall vase, closed her eyes and said a fervent prayer that the card would contain a message from Claudio. *Please God,* she prayed, *give me a sign, a direction, a path for my poor heart. Let them be from Claudio. Please.* She opened the tiny envelope with trembling hands.

Two words. She sighed; wrong flower, wrong man. Two words: *Love Paul.* Two words that dashed her hopes. Not a closing, nor a reminder, no comma, just a period after the name. She peered more closely. *Love Paul.* It was actually more of a command.

When she got home, the mail was waiting. A fat white envelope reminded her that her sister's wedding was in four weeks. She tapped the invitation, closed her eyes and pictured herself twirling around the dance floor with Claudio. On second thought, though it took great effort, she changed her dance partner to Paul.

"Do you ever wish we'd done it?"

Modesta started. She hadn't seen Paul, hadn't heard him come in. "I'm sorry, what did you say?" she automatically replied.

He threw his keys on the table, took the invitation from her and sat down. "Do you ever wish we'd waited? Had the big church wedding like Adela and Claudio did? Like Trini and BOB will?"

Modesta stamped a high-heeled foot. "Don't be silly. I'm not sentimental and I'm certainly not a good Catholic."

Paul looked up at her and for the first time she could remember, he had a wistful face. "You're my wild thing. Beautiful and free."

She drew him to his feet. "Your wild thing, anyway." She swayed in his arms, like they were dancing. "Oh, and thank you for the flowers. They were lovely."

"You're welcome." They kept dancing. "Hey, wait a minute, Monkey, I didn't send you flowers."

"Sure you did! Yellow roses. They're your fav..." She stopped.

"You know I don't send flowers." Paul twirled her. "Must have been from a grateful client."

"Oh, right." Modesta nodded.

In The Mercy We Bestow

"So, what's the plan?" Teb leaned over the bar toward María Elena. "First," he tapped his index finger, "It's gotta be someone who looks good in a tux..."

"Don't you worry about me! I'll think of someone to take to the wedding!"

"Sure you will! It's in a week, right? Plenty of time!"

"*Not* helping," María Elena muttered under her breath. She hurried to wait on a new table of boisterous middle-aged men. How could she have let this happen? Only a week left before her sister's wedding, and still she had no date. No prospects. All her friends were women – well, except for Nilo. No. She sighed. That would be leading him on...

"Hey," Teb laughed. "Don't slam the glasses! You'll break something!"

"Just because you own the bar doesn't mean you can yell at me every chance you get! Get Sheila to serve the drinks."

"Now, María Elena, you know I sell twice as much liquor when you're working! Don't be in a huff. Hey, *I* could always bail you out if..."

She ran off again. The last thing she wanted was to have Teb as her date. Her *boss?* That would be just perfect! Modesta would never let her forget it. And Teb? He would lord it over her. She'd have to quit her job, that's all. No, that was definitely *not* the solution.

Teb went right on polishing the liquor bottles. If his feelings were hurt, he never let on. María Elena returned with another drink order. "I meant I could schedule you to work that night – make it really important or something so you could skip the wedding altogether. That's all I was gonna say." He looked over her head in a very studied way.

"Oh. I thought..."

"Yeah, well, you think too much. Anyone ever tell you that?"

"And you think I could 'not go' to my own sister's wedding? I'm in it, remember? You don't think enough! Anyone ever tell *you* that?"

"Daddy, how come Auntie Mo and Uncle Paul didn't have a big wedding like you and Mama?"

Claudio laughed with a mouthful of salami sandwich. He shook his head. "How do you know that?"

Mercedes took her sandwich apart and folded the salami. "Everyone knows. It's what you call *common knowledge.*"

"I see," he said gravely.

"Anyway," she popped the meat into her mouth, "how come?"

Claudio shrugged. "Can you see your Aunt Modesta in a big white dress? I guess she and

Uncle Paul thought it much more romantic to run off, so that's what they did."

"Oh!" Mercedes considered this, chewing slowly. "But you and Mama thought it was more romantic to get married in church, with everyone around?"

"Yes. It was what your mama wanted. And her mamá. And mine."

"What about you?"

"I wanted to make your mama happy." He ruffled her hair, which she immediately smoothed again. "That's love."

"Will you take a date to Auntie Trini's wedding?"

"Aren't you going to be my date?"

Mercedes giggled. "I'm too young! Plus, we're related!"

He laughed. "But you're the best dancer I know!"

Mercedes shook her head solemnly. "Aunt Modesta is."

"Well, I'm related to her too. And she's married!"

Mercedes finished the salami and started on her bread. "Okay. You'll have to get me a corsage then. *Abuela* says a nice man gives a girl flowers to wear when he takes her dancing."

He crossed his arms. "Oh, she does, does she?"

"So, they say one day there will be no smoking in bars and restaurants and all like that." Teb lit his own cigarette as he passed on this bit of information to María Elena. She was sitting at he bar, indulging in her free employee drink, which Teb insisted she accept since they were closed and all alone. A group of people paused at the locked door, peered in. Teb waved them away and they stumbled on down the sidewalk. "Some people don't know when to quit!"

María Elena coughed. "That sounds extreme. What would it do to businesses like yours if no one was allowed to smoke?"

"Mine? Probably fold. Who wants to drown his sorrow, or celebrate, try to impress a chick, without one of these?" He blew smoke rings to make his point.

"Some people say that's just an extension of your..."

"Don't say it!"

"Ego." She giggled.

"Why don't you smoke?"

"Why should I?"

"I don't know. It's cool." Teb offered her one.

"Do you think leather jackets are cool?"

"Sure!"

"Then I'll take one of those, instead." She slid off her stool and went to the door. "See you tomorrow."

"So you're not asking him then." Teb was suddenly very busy rinsing out their glasses.

María Elena paused. "I'm not doing what?"

"You heard me."

She colored. "He wouldn't want to go."

Teb nodded. "So you're not asking him 'cause you feel sorry for him."

"No." She walked back to the bar and put her purse down. "I just don't think he wants to go to a wedding. It's the kind of thing he used to make fun of back when..."

"Back when he could dance?"

"Hey, just because he can't dance doesn't mean I don't want to be seen with..."

"No, I know, I know. You're not like that." Teb kept polishing the glass in his hand. He slid it into the glass rack and looked at María Elena. "Well, why not then? You gotta get used to it sometime if you're gonna hook up. I mean, sure you're used to seeing him in here and all but it's a big world, Sugar –"

"What did you just call me?"

"And you guys can't just hide out."

"What are you talking about?"

Teb was surprised that María Elena looked so genuinely baffled. "You and Nilo."

"Yeah?"

"Yeah. You know. As a couple."

"A what? Me and Nilo? Since when did we become a couple?"

"Since you told me to go after that Peaches chick to clear the way for you! Why do you think I hauled her crazy ass home the other night? Lemme tell you..."

"Oh, poor baby! The sacrifices you make for others. I swear, you're just like a saint."

He nodded solemnly. "Saint Stephen."

"Well, Saint Stephen, I'm afraid that was one sacrifice in vain." María Elena picked up her purse. She was suddenly exhausted.

Teb tried not to smile, not to feel the elation beginning to swell. "So you're not...?"

"We are not." She walked back to the door. "I only urged you to consider Peaches because Nilo asked me to. He wants you to settle down with someone, fall in love." She pulled the door open. "You know, he's convinced he's ruined your life." And with that dramatic statement she marched through the door.

Teb was paralyzed for a moment. "He ruined *my* life?" he repeated, with growing awe.

He walked to the door, watched the head-lights come on as her car pulled out of the parking lot. *Why didn't you do it?* a voice asked. It was a voice he knew well.

"Do what?" he murmured.

Ask her to let you be her date. You know you want to.

"Ah, what I want to do with that girl – I wouldn't know where to begin."

What are you talking about? Just another chick.

"Listen, my man, that one's something else." He rubbed his hands together. "So, she's not in love with Nilo?"

We should celebrate.

Teb went back to the bar. "Feel like getting drunk?"

"Mamá! What are you doing still up?" María Elena had entered the house as quietly as she could. The light was on in the living room, but all the bedrooms were dark. She had assumed everyone was sleeping.

"*Querida*, you should stay in the city, at Modesta's, when you are this late! Aren't you tired? How was work?"

María Elena dropped onto the sofa. "I don't like going to Modesta's anymore. She makes me feel sad. And besides, work wasn't so bad. I had a drink before I left, that's all."

Mamá raised her eyebrows. Before she could even say anything, María Elena leaned forward. "I know, I know, but sometimes you have to join in – for the other person."

"And is the other person an underage girl who is about to get in her car and drive all the way...?"

"Ok, ok, Mamá. I'm sorry. I won't do it again." She frowned. "Probably won't get much of a chance anyway. Poor Teb's worried that smoking's going to be outlawed and he'll go out of business."

Mamá narrowed her eyes. "And what about this Esteban?"

"What do you mean, Mamá? Teb's Nilo's brother. He's my boss. You know that."

"Is he single?"

María Elena rolled her eyes. "Not *him*, Mamá."

"Why not? You seem to like him."

"I'll admit there's something attractive about him. But he has that doomed thing..."

"What thing?"

María Elena sat up straight. "Mamá, he thinks he's not good enough for me. And you know, when a man thinks that way, he ends up convincing you of it in the end. That's all." She sat back again. "It's a doomed thing. Plus, he's never even asked me out. He mostly makes fun of me."

"Ah! Then he does like you."

María Elena laughed and kissed her mother on the top of her head. "Good night, Mamá. You forget I'm not in third grade. We don't just kick each other in the shins anymore."

"Sure you do." She chuckled. "And don't judge your sister Modesta. This wedding is not easy on her."

María Elena wondered why Trini's wedding would be hard on Modesta. Modesta was happily married, well–to-do, successful. Trini was next in line for marriage; it was her turn, after all. María Elena thought if this wedding were difficult for anyone, it would be so for Claudio. It would remind him of his own wedding and his lovely bride, her sister Adela. Adela died so unexpectedly. He still looked sad sometimes.

Trini was sitting up in bed. "Hey, you're home late!"

"And you're still awake. Shouldn't you be getting your beauty sleep?"

Trini giggled. "I guess it's too late for that!"

"Hey, Trini? What's up with Mo?"

Trinidad frowned. "What do you mean?"

"She's so, so..."

"Competitive? Bossy? Hell-bent on making you feel inferior to her in any way she can? Like you're not good enough – like..."

"Okay, okay!" María Elena started to undress. "But why? Why is she like that?"

Trini leaned on one elbow. "She always wanted to be the best. I don't know why. Even when we were kids, her doll was the rich one, the winning athlete, the famous movie star. Remember?"

María Elena on pulled a T-shirt for a nightgown and sat facing her sister. "But why would your wedding upset her?"

"Oh. That." Trini fell back onto the bed. "You really want to know?"

María Elena nodded.

"It makes me sound like a bitch, but she doesn't want me to be happier than she is. She's mad 'cause I'm marrying the man of my dreams."

"*BOB?*"

"I know, I know." Trini shook her head. "BOB."

"Doesn't she love Paul?"

Trini shrugged. "Beats me. Maybe she loves him, but not like that." She yawned. "No, not like that."

"He loves *her* like that."

Trini nodded. "Sometimes, often I think, one loves more than the other."

"Who loves who more with you guys?"

"Me and BOB?" Trini laughed. "That's the best part. I can't tell."

"Hey, Boss." The next day, María Elena dropped onto a stool next to Teb. He was seated at the bar, poring over a stack of paperwork.

"Hey," he muttered.

"How does it look?" She was amused.

"Grim." He took off a pair of glasses and rubbed his nose. Then he leaned his head on his hand and turned to look at her. "This is better."

She blushed. "Where's the insult?"

"Is that what I do?" He sounded sad.

"Sure. It's what we both do."

"Well, then, here's an idea." *Don't do it,* the familiar voice whispered. *Don't let the wall down. She'll see!* He shuddered. "What do you say we call a truce?"

María Elena considered this and a slow smile came to her face. "Okay," she said softly, extending her hand.

Bad move! Bad move, Idiot! You'll see!

"Shut up," Teb hissed.

"What?" María Elena asked.

"Nothing. I wasn't talking to you."

They shook.

María Elena hummed under her breath all day at work. The restaurant was busy.

"Say, Teb," she said fetching soft drinks for a family. "Why did you say things looked grim this morning? Business is great!"

His face softened. "Guess I had the wrong perspective. Things are looking better."

"Good, 'cause I have to talk to you about something. After the rush." She hurried back to wait on more customers before he could say anything else.

"Okay, what was so important?" The restaurant was nearly empty. Teb switched the tape to a classical one. Setting the mood. He tried to sound casual.

"Well, I'm not sure how to put this."

"Just ask it."

"Ask what?"

"Weren't you gonna ask me something?"

"Huh. Ask. Yeah, okay." María Elena spread her fingers on the bar and looked at them. She would need a manicure before the wedding. "I'm thinking about going to graduate school. To study English. But if I do, I'll need more money and fewer hours. Any way we can arrange that?"

"Oh." Teb turned around abruptly and hit his knee on a bottle of vodka. "Ow. Shit."

"You okay?"

Of course not. It wasn't the money, but he didn't want María Elena to work fewer hours, and more importantly, he didn't want that to be the question. The wedding was in two days. "Did you know I have my own tux?"

"What?"

"I'm just saying, I own a tuxedo. I look great in it, too."

"Um, that's nice, Teb. Guess you want to think about the grad school thing, huh?"

"Yeah. More thinking. That's what I want."

Teb suspected he shouldn't do it, but by the time he knew it was true, he was already in his car, headed toward her sister's house. They had worked late and María Elena said she was staying at Modesta's house. She was *right there* – mere blocks away – within reach. He couldn't resist.

You Idiot! I told you it wouldn't work! Being nicer to her isn't gonna get you anywhere! And now look at you!

"Shut up, God's sake!"

It's the rush isn't it? The chase – the longing. But what happens when you catch them? You lose interest. It gets boring. You have to untangle all that mess you worked so hard to weave.

"The rush," he mused.

But you won't catch this one. You can't soil her and throw her away. Not this one. This one, you're gonna love forever...

"What's he doing now?" Modesta swirled the wine in her glass, deliberately not looking out the window.

María Elena peeked between the curtains. "Looks like he's just sitting there."

"You think he's stalking you?"

"*Teb*?" María Elena hooted.

"Hey, keep it down. Paul is trying to sleep. He has to catch an early flight tomorrow!"

"Sorry."

"Let's examine the facts. A – he is your boss. B – he is single and handsome and he owns a restaurant, so he's got money."

"And...," María Elena continued, "he can have any girl he wants so why would he be after me? Teb doesn't even like me. He thinks of me as Nilo's friend."

"Oh? And why do you say that?" Modesta threw back the rest of her wine. "Sure you don't want to join me?"

María Elena shook her head. "He's always poking fun at me. We have nothing in common. And he can get any girl he wants!"

"That's the second time you said that." Modesta didn't look convinced. "Maybe it's like grade school – you know, a boy knocks you down or pulls your hair because he likes you?"

"Okay, Mamá. Except for one thing – we're not in grade school anymore."

"Why don't you ask him to the wedding and find out?"

"What?"

"Still sitting there?"

María Elena checked and nodded.

"Yeah, ask him to the wedding and if he says yes, you'll have your answer."

"Are you kidding me? All I'll have is the answer to whether or not he wants to go to a stupid wedding and show off in his tux, not an admission of his undying passion! And how do you think Trini will feel if I use her wedding for some kind of romantic experiment?"

"Man, you really do think too much, you know that? How's Trini gonna know?"

María Elena didn't answer. She just kept looking out the window. The room was dark, so Teb couldn't see the girls watching him. "It's kind of sad. Teb sitting out there all alone."

"Oh, yes. Stalking is a lonely occupation, no question about it."

"You're heartless, you know that?"

Modesta looked shocked, but it was too dark for María Elena to see. She finished her wine. "I'm going to bed."

"We can't just leave him out there! Can we?"

Modesta sighed. "You take all the fun out of it." Before María Elena could stop her, Modesta was off the couch and out the front door. She marched up to the car and knocked on the window. Surprised, Teb lowered it.

"Teb, right? As in, Esteban's?"

He nodded.

"Man of few words. I like that. She isn't coming out. She can't imagine what you're doing here since, as she says, you can get any girl you want so you couldn't possibly be interested in her!"

Teb was still silent.

Modesta leaned on the car door. Teb could see into her blouse, her perfumed cleavage beckoned him. He swallowed.

"Listen, Honey, your only chance with my sister is complete and total honesty. If you are in love with her, *really* in love with her, you'll have to prove it. And I mean prove it, not just to her, but also to my brothers and my father *and* me. Understand?"

Fear and wonder stirred deep within. He nodded again.

"Now, do us all a favor and go home."

Give Us Courage

"Too remote? I just heard an airplane flying over!"

"Yeah, I know. Unfortunate choice of locations. We have fifteen minutes to film this scene before the next...fifteen, right Tony?" A scruffy boy nodded, eyes glued to his camera. "Until the next one flies over. Okay, ladies! One more time! Places!"

"Who does this guy think he is?" Hands in the air, a short girl with wiry black hair turned to the director.

"The writer." They shared a look.

An exhausting day continued.

"Okay, if it's supposed to be morning, you can't have people walking around in evening clothes. And don't forget, that guy wasn't wearing an earring in the last scene, so for all intents and purposes, he wasn't pierced. Did he find an intergalactic mall somewhere?" The girl shoved unruly hair out of her eyes, gave comments, advice, direction in a matter-of-fact way, not really criticizing so much as reminding everyone that they were incredibly stupid. She wasn't pretty, but she was arresting. Carlos watched her, fascinated.

"So, who is that?" He asked a grip.

"Lolly."

"Lolly?"

"Lolly, Molly, Polly. O'Brien. Irish chick. They always find some nutty chick for the continuity thing."

"The what thing?"

"Continuity, man. You know. Stuff that goes together. And, stuff that doesn't!" Carlos still looked confused. The grip sighed. "Like, if your main character is in different outfits 'cause you're shooting parts of the same scene over two days, and it doesn't make sense when you're putting the film together, you know? She's supposed to catch that kind of stuff."

"Oh. Film continuity, you mean. They actually pay someone just to do that?"

"Hey, man, it can save a lot of freakin' money! Oops, sorry man, I mean, a shitload of money – for the producers." The grip nodded wisely. "You need a freakin' continuity chick, man."

"You need one," Carlos echoed.

Filming was a world like no other. Carlos thrilled to see his words come to life. It had been his dream since he was eleven to write stories and see them on the big screen. His family and friends were pleased, but not surprised. "Carlos has been writing his whole life! Of course he's good at it." Trini always shrugged in a matter-of-fact way. Nunzio took an even more casual attitude. "He better be good at it. Waste of his

God-damn life if he isn't!" But Modesta and María Elena and his mother and father were bursting with pride. "My little brother, a famous movie mogul!" was how Modesta liked to put it. Her husband, Paul, was more inclined toward Nunzio's way of thinking, but he wisely held his tongue.

The only one who wasn't pleased with the project was his best friend. BOB pressed his lips together to keep from screaming, "Is THAT what's important to you? Do you NEED the validation of a bunch of movie executives who measure success in dollars? Are you writing to give a lot of half-wit asses a reason to stare at a big screen for two hours, or are you writing to make the world a better place?" He often walked away when anyone brought up the name of Carlos Méndez.

This made things awkward for Trini. She loved her brother and her fiancé, but there was no way she could change the mind of either one. Knowing this, she didn't even try.

At lunchtime in the fifth week of filming, Carlos saw Lolly sitting alone, eating what looked like a tuna-salad sandwich. He walked over, tossing an apple back and forth between his hands.

"How's the continuity of the sandwich?" he asked with a self-deprecating grin.

Without looking at him she replied, "That supposed to be funny or rhetorical?"

"You always answer a question with a question?"

"You always ask such stupid questions?"

"May I join you?"

"It's still a free country, isn't it?"

"Are you this competitive, or simply addicted to playing games?"

"What you know about playing games?"

"What's a guy gotta do to get a straight answer from you?"

"What's being straight got to do with it?"

"Are you?"

"Aren't you?"

Carlos burst into a laugh and dropped down beside her. "You win. I'm straight."

"Loser. That was rhetorical. How the hell could you be anything but straight?" She picked at her tuna.

"Here we go again. Carlos Méndez. Writer." He stuck out a hand.

"Would you believe, Lolly O'Brien?" She brushed the hair from her eyes and proceeded to finish her sandwich in silence. Carlos watched her walk away when she was done. Her tight little jeans and white tank top disappeared around a corner. He wondered what it would be like to walk down Mamá's hill with her on his arm. Carlos bit into his apple. "Well, that was weird," he muttered, and immediately he began wondering what she thought of him.

"Carlitos, you're not tasting." Mamá shook a finger at him. "Big famous writer now, eh? You can't taste the stew for your own mother?"

"Mamá, Mamá!" Carlos laughed and blushed. "I've just got so much on my mind, with the movie and all." He quickly dug into a thick beef stew with his favorite, tortillas. "Um, this is good," he mumbled with his mouth full. "Trini and BOB coming?"

"Yes, yes, of course." Modesta interrupted. "It wouldn't be a family dinner without those two glow-worms! Fiancés – ugh!"

"Now Modesta, we were that way once upon a time." Paul tried to feed his lovely wife a bite of his stew.

She backed away. "Whoa, whoa there, mister! This is silk, are you crazy?" She covered her blouse with her hands in horror.

"A long time ago," he murmured.

Mamá gave her a look, but Modesta kept her eyes on her blouse, frantically scrubbing at an imaginary stain.

"Hey! We're here! Where are you guys hiding?" Everyone burst into a laugh, as the house was much too small to hide anyone. BOB and Trini waltzed in, BOB obediently carrying a tray of something for the party. He kissed Mamá on the cheek.

"Trini cooked."

"Ah!" Mamá smiled, took the pan and, lifting a corner of aluminum foil, sniffed suspiciously. "What did she cook?"

"Lasagna! But it got burnt, somehow, so this is spaghetti and meatballs from the market." Everyone laughed as Trini gave BOB a playful shove.

"Well, at least I tried!"

"Thank you, dear." Mamá gave her a hug. "But remember to keep it simple. Lasagna is hard for a beginner. Must you be so grand?"

The dog barked outside. María Elena said, "You should have brought it anyway – for Cucho."

"I thought you liked that dog?" BOB laughed as Trini punched him again. "Ow! You're gonna hurt me one of these days."

"All the more reason to behave yourself, Mr. Simon."

"Point taken, Soon-to-be Mrs. Simon."

The family continued to laugh and banter as Mamá issued orders to Trini and María Elena about the food, and Modesta rearranged the centerpiece.

Carlos waited until BOB was alone on the porch, having a smoke. "Hey, BOB."

"Carlos. Movie going well?"

"Like you care."

"I do."

"Yeah, okay. It's going okay, I guess."

"What's wrong?"

"What do you mean?'

"Cut the crap. Something's on your mind." BOB took a long drag and watched Carlos intently as he exhaled.

"I, um..." Carlos frowned. "I need your advice."

"I already told you to quit bastardizing your work for the masses."

"Not that. Not about that."

"What then?" BOB squinted at him. He had never seen Carlos nervous. He looked thinner too. "Hey, you okay?"

Carlos ran his hand through his hair. "Remember that day we were dropping rocks from the bridge? *Milagros?*"

BOB laughed. "Yeah. That was the day I asked your permission to take your sister out." BOB took another long drag. "Holy...whoa!" he coughed. "Don't tell me you're in love! Ha! Never thought I'd see the day. Now you know what it's like. You finally know the desperate ravaging pain that is love. And you're ready to forgive me now for wrecking our friendship?"

"What in God's name are you talking about?"

"Oh. It's something else then?"

Carlos looked off into the woods. "No. It's love all right."

"And?" BOB kept smoking.

"And, I guess I didn't know you thought I was still mad at you. I mean, c'mon, pretty soon you'll be my brother. But it isn't about that."

"You gonna tell me what it is?"

"It's the craziest thing. Really, I'm completely lost! I don't have the tiniest idea how to get her. She doesn't even notice me, doesn't know I exist. I sat right across from her at lunch one day and it was like I wasn't even there."

"She on the crew? An actress? What?"

"Continuity girl."

"What girl?"

"Continuity. Looks for gaps in the story, time of day, clothing, age, year, etc. She keeps it real."

"Huh." BOB nodded. Carlos wasn't the type to go after a girl for the sake of a conquest and, like it or not, this one sounded like a conquest.

"Now, I wouldn't call you a regular Romeo," Carlos continued, "you know, a lady killer or anything."

"Think you'll get better advice if you insult me first?" BOB raised an eyebrow.

"No, no. What I mean is, well, you got Trini. That's no small thing. She was practically engaged to that all-star, perfect guy, old what's his name."

"Ken."

"Yeah, Ken. And then you came strolling along and plucked her right out of his hand! I never told you, but that was part of what made me so mad at you. I mean, it was so easy for you. How'd you do it?" Carlos was red in the face.

"Hold on now! Your sister wasn't a prize to be plucked. She was my other half. The magnet is drawn to the metal too. Is this girl your other half?"

Carlos bit his lip. "Could be."

"Well then, all you have to do is figure out what she wants."

"Oh, that's all, is it?"

"Yep. And that's the easy part. Then you have to figure out how to give it to her so she doesn't know you're giving it to her and when she's ready to drop from surprise, all you have to do is be there to catch her." BOB smiled. "That's all."

"Oh, man! You make it sound like one of your crazy games."

"It is. But the payoff is unbelievable."

Modesta was watching Trinidad stir a pot filled with pinto beans and a big ham hock. Trini was frowning with the effort. The steam from the pot made her already frizzy hair form little curls around her forehead.

"How do you like being engaged?" Modesta asked.

"I love it." The tone of her voice emphasized the simple phrase. Trini's eyes held a glow that Modesta hadn't noticed before.

"Funny," she murmured. "I don't remember being like that."

Trini kept her eyes on the beans. "It was a long time ago for you."

"Still... Hey, how come I always see you in those pearl earrings?"

"They're my favorites. BOB gave them to me."

"So that's all you're ever gonna wear now?"

"Well, sure. Until he gets me something else. But you know what they say about pearls; the more you wear them, the greater their luster."

"Yeah, sure, but I'll keep my diamonds, thank you." Modesta fingered her own ear lobe.

Trini gave a glance that took in her sister's entire ensemble: silk, diamonds, high-heeled boots. Trini's black jeans and sweater that had looked so sharp in BOB's little two-bedroom house, now seemed childish. She pushed the spoon harder, determined not to care.

And all Modesta saw when she looked at her sister was the happy, contented person Trinidad had become. No money, no plan, just a woman who was about to marry the man she loved. How did that work, she wondered? "Well, pearls suit you," she finally acquiesced.

"Why do you always do that?" Trini asked quietly.

"Do what? You look good in pearls, that's all!"

"No. You know what I mean. You always have to compare us. You have to beat me. Why must everything be a contest?"

"I have no idea what you're talking about!" Modesta stood straighter, picked up her glass of wine and drank.

"Especially since I got engaged," Trini continued. "It's like you always have to reassure yourself that you're still the one who's better off."

"Don't be silly."

"Don't you wear jewelry because Paul gave it to you?"

Modesta had to think. Did Paul give these to her? Her hand flew up to her ear again. "Of course! He just has better ..."

Trini put the spoon down. "Better taste than BOB? More money? A better job, better car, bigger house?"

"I was going to say better connections. He has friends in the diamond trade and he gets things at a discount that..." But Trini was already walking away.

"Trinidad! You turned those beans off, didn't you?" She could hear Mamá's voice in the distance. "They'll burn."

"I got it, Mamá!" Modesta hurried to the stove and turned off the flame under the beans. She gave the pot a stir, just for good measure. A little splash dotted her silk blouse, but she didn't notice.

"So it's another game," Carlos repeated. He was sitting next to BOB on the porch, watching him smoke. BOB nodded.

"Best game of your life. I only wish I'd invented it." He looked at his friend. For the first time ever, Carlos appeared anxious, unsure of himself. "This girl must be something else!"

Carlos whistled. "You know how when you're out in public and you do something really stupid, like falling on a patch of ice or something? And you're suddenly filled with a mix of anger and shame but the overall sensation is one of embarrassment and it's so ridiculous that all you can do is laugh and that's even more embarrassing?"

BOB nodded. "You've just described my life from thirteen to the day I met your sister."

"Well, other than the actual bruising, that's how I feel every time I see this girl. Woman. Girl."

"Okay. Let's break it down."

"Coffee."

BOB gave Carlos a blank look.

"She's always drinking coffee when I see her."

"Oh. Black? Cream? Sugar?"

"Cream. Definitely cream. She spilled some the other day and it definitely had cream in it."

"Sugar?"

"Doubt it. She's a runner, you know, into health and stuff."

"What does she eat for lunch?"

"Only a sandwich. But a big sloppy sandwich – tuna, hummus, that kind of thing."

"Okay, what else?"

"She's always reading."

"Work or pleasure?"

"Um, both. She doesn't talk a lot."

"Hold on. What kind of reading?"

"Looks like classics from the cover. I have to work on that one."

"Music?"

"Beats me."

"That's enough to start."

"Start what?"

"Your strategy. Number one: coffee. Did you ever hear of a coffee drinker who wasn't completely blown away by that rocket fuel your dad makes in his glass pot? Take a thermos to work. Tomorrow. With cream in it. Number two: sandwiches. You still eat those avocado and tomato sandwiches with the chips? Make one with whole grain or baked or whatever kind of healthy chip you can find. Number three: buy one of those running magazines and be reading it when she walks by."

"I said she reads classic stuff!"

"You also said she runs. And you better get in shape. Oh, I know! Start writing a film about running or a runner, or write a story. She reads. You write. Should be a match made in heaven!"

"Or Borders."

"Ha."

"Hey, Trini, I'm sorry." Modesta found Trini looking out the window, spying on her fiancé and her brother.

"Sh!"

"What are you doing?"

"I think they're finally making up!"

"Who? What?" Modesta looked too. Carlos and BOB were laughing together, drinking beer, their voices rising and falling. Trini's face was full of delight. "Do you still get that feeling every time you look at him?" Modesta asked.

"BOB? I still can't believe he wants to marry me." Trini twirled the ring on her finger.

"Why do you say that? You're a catch!"

"Ha! You were the catch, not me."

"Trini, I didn't mean..."

"Hey, you ever wonder whatever happened to Luis?"

"You mean the carpenter?"

"Yeah."

"The one who hardly ever spoke and liked to cook and had to hang drywall all winter cause work was so slow?"

"Yeah. Him. Do you ever wonder about him?"

"That was even before I met Claudio," Modesta mused. "No. Not really."

"He used to make you laugh."

"He used to make faces at me all the time."

"Luis. Mamá liked him."

"Mamá likes everyone."

"She likes everyone who makes us happy. You guys were sweet together. He picked flowers for you and he came over to take out your garbage. And you knitted him that scarf, that horrible purple scarf, and he wore it all that winter, remember?"

"I remember he had no money to buy flowers and I had no money to buy him a birthday gift. He lived above a bar, for goodness sake!"

"And you used to sit on the roof of that bar with him and he'd play the guitar and you'd sing."

"Oh, yeah! Funny, how you forget stuff..."

"I guess there was some stuff you don't want to remember." Both girls were silent, then Trini continued softly, "But if he'd had the courage to marry you, I bet you'd know how I feel."

"Is that so?" Shame and remorse seeped through a small crack in Modesta's carefully built armor. She stiffened.

Trini pictured her sister, with a little more weight and a lot less makeup, her hair long and loose, eyes always tilted in a smile. What if she hadn't had the abortion? What if she'd married Luis and raised a new baby every year? She would have had an ordinary life, a beautiful, magical, ordinary life. She could have welcomed old age with children and grandchildren and a man who adored her...

But of course she wanted more – as if there was more.

Modesta glared out the window at the boys, who were still talking. "Don't kid yourself," she said. "You're making a rash decision, marrying that boy. What kind of a provider, or husband or father for that matter, do you think he will be?"

Trini looked sober. "I don't know. But Mamá once said, when a man has nothing but his heart to give and he gives it, he's giving you all he has."

On Tuesday, Carlos tried to look casual as he searched the set for Lolly. He was armed with a coffee.

On further speculation, he had decided to grab a coffee from the gas station he passed on his way to work. How could he ask his father for a pot of coffee without going into great detail about its purpose? Then the internal debate about one coffee or two was easy. One would be easier to camouflage if she turned him down. Turned the coffee down. Where was she? He nearly threw the scalding beverage in the trash. What was wrong with him? Was this Carlos Méndez? Trailing after some goofy chick just to ply her with coffee in the vain hope that she...

He turned a corner and there she was.

Lolly O'Brien was in a dress. A dress? A white gauzy thing with a flowing skirt, cinched at the waist. Such a tiny waist. How could a delicate creature like that be insensitive to his advances?

"You stupid jerk! I told you on Friday, 'Don't forget to keep that outfit dirty! You just motored across a sea of mud! Do NOT wash those clothes!' Look at you! If you were any cleaner you'd be Goddamn Mr. Clean! I mean, you WOULD BE Mr. Clean! You're so white you look like Casper! You're too clean for clean! Get outta here! Screw the scene! Where's the director?"

Carlos saw his cue. "Coffee?"

Lolly grabbed it and took a gulp. "Ugh! Hot! Excellent." She turned away immediately and went in search of the director.

At lunchtime, Carlos made sure to be in the courtyard where Lolly usually ate. He unwrapped a thick sandwich of avocado and tomato and proceeded to ignore it as he perused the latest copy of *Runner* magazine. An hour-and-a-half later he succumbed to hunger and nearly threw the magazine away, until he remembered he would need it again, tomorrow.

The next day Carlos had to drink the coffee himself, but lunch was more successful. He adopted his casual air and actually was drawn to an article about extreme sports, when he sensed someone standing next to him. He looked up.

"You a runner?" She was wearing scrubs today. (She even looked good in scrubs!)

"You?"

"Do I seem like one?"

"What does one seem like?"

"Am I fit?"

"Fit for what?"

"For a woman my age, height, weight, nationality, occupation?"

"Religion and political persuasion?"

"Well?"

He stood. "Do you like avocado sandwiches?"

"Aren't they high in fat?"

"You worried about fat?"

"Isn't everybody?"

"Doesn't it get tiresome?"

"What?"

"Playing this game. There. That's not a question." Carlos sat down, picked up the sandwich and handed Lolly half. "Must we always compete?"

"Isn't that a question?" She bit into her half. But she didn't leave.

Carlos just shrugged. "What is it you want?"

Lolly kept eating, chewing slowly, as if she were considering her answer. "What do you mean?"

"I mean, what is it that keeps you going? What makes you get up in the morning? What do you hope to attain? Does this job fulfill some kind of dream? Some aspiration? Are you happy or hopeful or what?"

She sat. She kept eating and locked eyes with him. "How can I answer all that with my mouth full?" she mumbled, a crumb threatening to fall from her lip.

He lowered his eyes, hiding his triumph from her. "You just can't do it, can you?"

She swallowed and smiled. He had never seen her smile. What a glorious parting of lips, ever to light up a face! And her eyes crinkling at their corners and the way her nose turned up. What a face! What a moment! Suddenly he believed without any doubt, this was worth all the playing he would have to do.

Entrust Our Days
And Nights To You

María was finally able to walk outdoors. She stood in the dirt yard, inhaled the hot air, smiled as the sun baked her arms, her face. For a moment she was happy just standing there, the agony of lying in bed wrapped in pain a distant memory, like a garment she was finally able to shed.

Her illness had been a nightmare. The muffled sounds, endless nights, tasteless food. Of course, there had been Manuel, so sweet, so attentive. She frowned. And his kindness was the only lingering discomfort.

So many times she'd opened her eyes, it was surely the middle of the night, and there he would be, asleep in the chair next to her bed. If she didn't love him so, she would have been frightened at the similarity of this to her own vigil over Rafaela. He wiped her brow, smiled and talked and pretended that she was only resting, not wasting away with illness. At times, she had been so sure that he loved her. But then what happened?

She rubbed her forehead. What was it he'd said? It was last Wednesday, she was sure. She wanted to tell him she was feeling a little better, but then he said something about a calling and she'd been so surprised – shocked into silence. Mamá and Papá never spoke of it to her... wouldn't they have known? Could she have dreamed it, or was it true?

"María!" As if thinking of him must have summoned him, Manuel was suddenly in front of her, standing with his mouth open, his hands spread wide. "Look at you! What are you doing out here? Are you cold? Here." He took off his hat and jammed it on her head, her hair flowing like a cape around her shoulders. Her dress hung loosely; her feet, as always, bare.

"Cold?" María shaded her eyes and squinted up at the bright sun above them. She forced a laugh. He looked like a priest already, dressed in black with a broad brimmed hat. She touched the hat lightly. "How do I look?"

Standing in the yard, thinner, paler, but with that mischievous sparkle back in her eye, she was adorable to Manuel. He blushed. "Ah, it is good to see you so well again!"

She cast her eyes down. This was not what she hoped to hear. She shook her head; her hair swished around her shoulders. "And where have you been, sir? School and work must keep you ever busy. I've been well for days now, and you never knew."

Manuel's eyes grew round. "When?" he demanded, "When did you begin to improve?"

"Oh," she skipped lightly around him, "it's funny, you know? I remember exactly because you had just been to see me and it was after you left; it was last week, Tuesday. I felt the fever lift and with it, the pain. It disappeared. Suddenly. Just like that." María snapped her fingers. "I meant to tell you before..."

"Last week, Tuesday," he echoed. He whistled, scraping the dirt with the toe of his shoe.

"What?" María said curiously.

Manuel shook his head. "Nothing, nothing. Look, I have to go, I, ah, I was just checking on you." He faced her, placed his hands on her shoulders. "You are better then," he said simply, sadly.

"But you don't have to leave," she said hurriedly.

"I, I have a class."

"Oh? What is it?" She touched his arm.

He looked where her fingers lay. "Apostolic Theology."

She nodded. "Then it's true."

"I told you."

"I thought perhaps I'd dreamed it."

He looked down. "It is a good thing, María. And now you will live."

"Ah, *sí*." She turned away so he wouldn't see her eyes fill with tears.

He suspected her pain and marveled at her self-control. It took all his strength to walk away that day, he thought perhaps for the last time.

Weeks went by. María continued to grow stronger and Manuel continued his studies.

"Manuel!" Father Eber gestured to his young student one day. "Come here, Son."

"Yes, Father?" Manuel hurried over and bowed, ever respectful of the old priest's ways.

"I need help with this." He motioned toward the weeds flourishing in his garden. "The rake is behind the barn."

Manuel went to fetch it and when he returned the old priest was on his knees, weeding, tearing out the unwanted greens and gently stroking the vegetables that now had room to grow.

"Here, Father. Let me." Manuel joined him and vigorously pulled the rake through the soil, turning over the dirt, breaking big clumps and separating weeds from plants, his fingernails filling with dirt.

"Easy, easy, Son. You do have the enthusiasm of youth!" Father Eber chuckled. When Manuel did not laugh with him, the Father frowned and sat back on his heels. He picked apart a flower that was brown on the edges, though it was still young. "Do you see this? When a new blossom curls up this way, loses its fine color and begins to dry on the edges, something is eating it from the inside. By the time we notice, the damage is already done."

Manuel nodded.

"Our seminary garden is very dear to us. We cannot tend it properly without the reassurance that each member is strong and well within." He looked into Manuel's eyes.

"Ah, *sí.*" Manuel murmured, blushing.

"My son, true joy comes from fulfilling our purpose. Where is yours?"

"My happiness is not important, Father."

"No. Not happiness. There is a difference between happiness and joy. If you are not truly called to the priesthood – if you are avoiding something, running from something in your life – this is no place to hide. We are a journey, not a sanctuary. Once begun, this journey does not stop, so you must be very sure before you embark, eh?"

Manuel dug deeply into the earth. He scooped great handfuls of soil and squeezed until the dirt came out between his fingers. "How can I, how can anyone...?" He shook his head.

"Oh, one can be sure." Father Eber tapped his chest. "You know it. The Lord speaks in many ways and one of those ways is with words. When He speaks, you are sure." His dark eyes were steady, implacable. "Tell me, Manuel, how did He speak to you?"

"Father," Manuel knelt in the garden. He did not look at the old priest. "Father, I asked the Lord to restore someone I loved and in exchange for this, I offered my own life."

"A living sacrifice?"

"*Sí.*"

The Father nodded, bent over and scooped up the discarded weeds. "You promised to become a priest?"

"Well, no, not exactly. That is, I didn't say the word priest, but I did offer my life, and this is the best way to serve Him, is it not?"

"Ah, well, if one is called to it, it is. To me and to priests and brothers all over the world it is, but not to all people." He smiled at Manuel.

"There are many ways to serve the Lord. Many journeys."

Together they carried the weeds to a compost heap behind the outdoor ovens. The old priest put his hands on his hips. "And what of this person whom the Lord restored? What is her journey?"

"Father, she is so, so..." Manuel looked at him now, locked his grave eyes upon the father's, not surprised that he had guessed it was a woman.

"Beautiful?"

Manuel nodded. "Of course, but not like that. She is brave and humble and she doesn't ask anything for herself. She suffered silently, not wishing to trouble anyone with her distress."

"True beauty, eh?" He chuckled, then grew severe. "Manuel, is there another obstacle? Is this woman married, or promised to another?"

"No, Father, no! María is neither married nor promised. In fact," he hesitated, "I believe she may never marry now."

Father Eber raised his eyebrows.

"I was," Manuel cleared his throat. "I was married to her sister once."

"Oh?"

"She is with the Lord nearly five years, now."

The father handed Manuel a hoe and they returned to the garden. "You did not wish to follow tradition, then?"

"I was confused. Oh, Father Eber, I thought I didn't love her as I ought. I was still in love with my wife. I hesitated and..."

"And she grew ill and you made a deal with our Lord and here you are."

Manuel nodded, for the first time seeing he may have mistaken his promise for a calling.

Father Eber leaned upon his rake. "My son, there will be many opportunities to sacrifice for the Lord, sacrifices you cannot know. When one commits to earthly love, to a wife and children, one becomes vulnerable to disappointments unimaginable. It is a sacrificial state, indeed. This kind of commitment also honors God when undertaken with a sober, holy intent." Father Eber went back to his hoeing, motioned Manuel to do the same.

They worked silently, Manuel wondering whether, in his fervor, he had taken a misstep. Priesthood wasn't a greater sacrifice? He chewed his lip. He knew it wasn't sanctuary. No, it was a commitment like any other. He stopped hoeing suddenly and looked at Father Eber. "Oh, Father! And what of María? Have I injured her with my heroics?"

The father smiled as he worked. "Not yet, my boy. There is still time to change your mind."

That In Pursuit of

Heaven's Honor

"I'll pick you up at seven. Here, or at your place?"

"How 'bout my place?" Lolly scribbled her address on a scrap of paper. "Seven-thirty?" She fidgeted with the pencil.

"Sure. Be hungry."

"Aren't I always?" She stood and looked down at him, her lips toying with a smile. "You like to tell people what to do, don't you?"

Carlos pushed back his chair. "I'd like the chance to tell you what to do, yes!" He jumped up and kissed her on the cheek. "Seven-thirty."

"What the...?" The address Lolly had given Carlos led to an old warehouse. He looked around. It appeared deserted. He wanted to knock, but didn't know exactly where. A tiny shower of dust or dirt or something like it sprinkled onto his head.

"Don't look up!"

He looked up. "Ow!" and brushed grit from his eyes.

"I'll be right down."

Carlos dusted himself off. From somewhere deep within the building he heard a jarring noise, followed by a screech. A metal door rolled open. There stood Lolly, crisp, sparkling, in another impossibly white gauze dress, hair cascading about her thin shoulders, hoop ear- rings, with a tiny diamond charm. "Sorry 'bout that. How come you looked up?"

"You told me not to." He smiled.

She smiled back with a very knowing look.

They went to the South Side and ate at a fancy Spanish restaurant. Lolly whistled. "You bring all your dates here?"

Carlos pulled out her chair. "Just the ones I like best."

"Oh-ho! Giving me the advantage so early?"

"Doesn't the girl always have the advantage?"

"Do you call waiting to be asked an advantage?"

"Depends on what you're waiting to be asked. You think it's more advantageous to be the beggar?"

"You have to beg?"

He laughed. *"Touché!"* They ordered wine and appetizers. Carlos watched, fascinated, as Lolly sucked the flesh from a shrimp, its tiny tail grasped firmly between her polished fingertips.

"Here." She held one to his lips. He obediently opened them. Ugh! He really didn't like shrimp.

"Thank you," he mumbled, covering his mouth with his napkin. "So, how did you get into this continuity thing?"

"Oh, compulsive obsession, I guess. Y'know, how it drives you crazy when people use incorrect grammar, or their shoes don't go with their outfits, like, they still wear earth shoes?"

"And just being that irritable gave you a career path?"

"Something like that." She blushed.

"Huh."

"You?"

"I wouldn't say I'm irritable. Observant, maybe. Tenacious. Focused. And I do love words."

"A born writer."

"Something like that."

"What's your favorite movie?" She went back to sucking on shrimp.

"Of all time? Let's see, I loved *The Crying Game; E.T.; The Way We Were; Sex, Lies and Videotape...*"

"*The Way We Were?*"

Carlos laughed. "Just wanted to see if you were paying attention!"

Lolly shook her head.

"You?"

"I hate movies."

"But they're your work!"

"They're my work. Got a favorite book?"

He nodded. "You?"

In unison, they said, "The dictionary."

"Oxford or Webster's?" Carlos raised an eyebrow.

She looked into his eyes as she replied, "Oxford," and faintly nodded.

After dinner they walked down Carson Street to a club, an old seedy place with a green awning and a sweaty smell. It was nearly empty, though several toughs were gathered at the far end of the bar. Lolly and Carlos took a table by the window and Carlos excused himself to go to the men's room.

"Hey, man!" One of the toughs with long hair and a leather vest turned to Carlos as he returned to the bar. "See that chick over there in the see-through dress? She just bet ..."

Carlos was pulling his fist from the man's face before he could finish his sentence. He glanced back at Lolly, standing in front of the window, the streetlight behind her, in that impossible dress. Lolly lifted her hair from the back of her neck, stepped up to the bar and beckoned to the bartender. "We'll have two cabernets on..." she pointed to the long-haired fellow, picking himself up from the floor "...that gentleman!"

"What did you do?" Carlos hissed. Lolly faced him, balancing on the dirty rail that circled the bottom of the bar. He could almost see her breasts, poised beneath the gauzy white top, almost imagine the lace on her panties, snug against firm white flesh. She grasped the bar behind her and leaned forward.

"Honestly, what's a girl supposed to do when a fellow waits for her date to go to the men's room and then hits on her? I couldn't very well punch him in the nose myself, could I?" Carlos fumed. "All I said was, 'If you so much as ac-knowledge me, my boyfriend will knock you down!' and he said, 'Wanna bet?' and I did!"

Lolly tried to look demure. "And, I won." She handed Carlos a glass of red wine.

He was mad enough to throw the wine on her pretty white dress, but the word "boyfriend" had hypnotized him, so he drank it instead.

When he took her home, Carlos walked Lolly to her door, her warehouse door. "You actually live here?"

She unlatched a metal hook, rolled the door to the side. He could see a staircase behind her, lit with mauve colored nightlights. "Why not? I have to live somewhere, don't I?" She laughed at him. "Want to come up for a nightcap?"

He marveled at the way she carried on a conversation, almost entirely with questions. Smiling, so she wouldn't know he was angry, he shook his head. The face of that longhaired biker, picking himself up from the floor, kept coming to mind. *What kind of a girl does that to a man?*

Lolly started to pout, but suddenly changed her mind. She lifted her face for a kiss. His arms went round her. Her waist was so small! His lips fell on hers and for a moment the heat of her body caught his on fire. He leaned into her, felt her breasts heave beneath that flimsy white dress. She took a step back. He let go.

"This is our first date."

"Ah, you play by the rules." She shrugged, lightly ran up the stairs, leaving Carlos to pull the door shut. Lolly was surprised when he didn't follow. "This one's a puzzle," she murmured to herself.

Carlos didn't see her on the set the next day. Relieved, he stayed in the background, just watching. That afternoon he took some notes to the library. The quiet, the solitude, soothed him. He had balanced a dictionary, a thesaurus and a legal pad on his lap, where he scribbled away until a shiny object – a copper painted stone – dropped onto his pad. He looked up.

"Penny for your thoughts."

"Hey!"

BOB pulled up a chair. "So, how goes it? You figure it out yet?"

Carlos scratched his head. "I'm trying another sci-fi thing, but it keeps getting medieval on me. Think that's a conflict?"

"Isn't it supposed to be?"

Carlos smiled. "Yeah, kinda." He leaned back in his chair. "What are you doing here?"

"I had some stuff to return and then I saw you. You don't look too happy."

"Ha! Coming from you..."

"Yeah, yeah, I know. What's up with the girl?"

Carlos blanched.

"There's my answer."

"Man, I think there's something...I don't know...off."

"What?"

"The game."

"What's her version?"

"I don't know! I think I'm supposed to chase her, then she lets me catch her, just a little, just enough to keep me coming back for more. She lures other men into it too. Maybe to make me jealous. Up the ante."

BOB nodded. "Sounds like she's playing 'The Rich Man And The Beggar.'"

"What are you talking about? You know I'm not rich!"

"No, man. She's the rich man and you're the beggar. See, the beggar will always want what the rich man has, so he tries to appear rich."

Carlos nodded, his mouth a little open.

"But the truth is, the reality of the situation is that the rich man wants what the beggar has, so he's constantly trying to lure the beggar to him. He can use jealousy, danger, wit, intellect, sexuality, whatever he thinks makes him most attractive. I mean 'her' of course."

"Oh, man. You should write a book!" To BOB's look of condescension, Carlos just smiled. "I mean another book. One about this stuff." He sighed. "Okay. You better tell me."

BOB squirmed. "Tell you what?"

"How do I win." Carlos set his lips in a line.

"Sorry, man. The beggar can't win this one.

He doesn't really want what the rich man has. It really is the other way around."

"Damn." Carlos laughed. "And she's playing so hard – so seriously! Like it's real."

"Huh. And it's not, right?"

"Not for me. I want something really real. Know what I mean?"

"Yeah. I think I do." BOB's smile wasn't a grimace this time.

A few days later, Lolly found Carlos, absently drinking a coffee using the runner's magazine as a giant coaster.

"Hey, where's mine?"

He looked up. "Your what?"

"My coffee. You didn't get me one today?"

"Here." He handed her his. "I don't really drink coffee." She took it and sat beside him.

"What about Saturday?"

"Can't. I'm tied up all day."

"All day and all night?"

He nodded. "Big family thing. My sister's wedding."

"Oh."

"Don't even think it."

"Think what?"

"I can't take you."

"Oh. You already have a date?"

"No." He shook his head. "You just don't get it."

She cleared her throat. "Maybe I'd like to."

He pictured her meeting his family, competing with Modesta's looks, with María Elena's youth, with Trini's happiness. And all she had for a weapon was her weird pixie charm. He saw Mamá's raised eyebrows, Father's grave smile. It wouldn't work.

Carlos took both her hands, impossibly small, pinkish white. "You're a lot like my sisters. Trini's really independent. And she has hair like yours." He didn't touch it. He knew if he did, he'd get caught, tangled up in it. "You have things in common with all of them, really. You've got Modesta's fierceness, María Elena's brains, but there's something missing. You don't have what

Adela had. What they all try to have. It doesn't take much, but without it, well..."

"What are you talking about? What don't I have?"

"Something to believe in. You have a big empty warehouse and a make-believe job. You need something real."

"You're real, aren't you?"

Carlos stood up. "But you can't have me. I won't play." He walked to the trashcan, threw in the magazine.

Lolly sat very still, for once at a complete loss.

Carlos didn't return to the set. The movie debuted and *Glorious Pursuit* was hailed as a great first effort. The critics called it simple but discerning, sensitive rather than sentimental. The perfect blend of myth and emotion. They gave it four-and-a-half stars out of five.

We May Celebrate, Ever Grateful

The sun rose as it did every day. Birds sang. The paperboy's aim was true. He hit the screen door, knocking the paper right through the screen. As though on cue, the noise jolted Trini upright in her bed. She gathered the blankets to her chin, whispered, "Today I'm getting married," then tossed the covers away and leaped onto her sister's bed. "Hey, I'm getting married! I'm getting married!" She shouted and bounced, forcing María Elena to bounce with her.

"Alright already," María Elena laughed. "I get it! You're getting married."

"Today. Come for a run with me," Trini ordered.

"Oh dear." María Elena flopped back on the pillow. "Now?"

"Yes, now! What a great way to start what shall always be remembered as 'The Day Trinidad Méndez Got Married.'"

"Yeah, that's what we need. Another day to celebrate in September!"

All of the Méndez children were born in September, the month of change. Three years ago, in the coldest September anyone could remember, one had died. Modesta and Paul had chosen this month to elope. And Mamá and Papá had married nearly forty years ago next week, unknowingly starting what would become a tradition of the Méndez family honoring September with every occasion under their command.

This day was cold and the sky soon darkened, portending a shower before long. The girls didn't notice. They ran blithely along, aware only that their hearts were light and they were young and full of life.

Trinidad loved to run, her muscled legs moving like wheels beneath her hips. María Elena, not a runner, did her best to keep up with her older sister. Periodically Trini would shout her news to a stranger, startling an old man out of his daydream, a woman and her dog from their morning routine, with the glad tidings, glorious miracle: she was getting married later that day! María Elena laughed. She shook her head over the strange things happiness does to people.

At five o'clock everyone gathered at the old church. Never mind the cold, the damp; Trini and BOB possessed a joy that radiated warmth throughout the room. The girls were all in lavender – Candelaria, six months pregnant with her round little belly, and her expectant glow; Modesta, breathtaking in curls piled high on her head and perfect makeup. Lavender became her.

María Elena, hair twisted into a French knot, a string of pearls circling her throat; she was a princess masquerading as a regular girl. Her beauty was not as flashy as Modesta's and Candelaria's. Hers was regal.

And the bride – the spiritual centerpiece of this sacramental occasion – Trinidad glowed with celestial joy. All her senses told her she was finally doing what was in accordance with the Lord's plan for her. Her total belief in this, and in her love, allowed whatever she wore to glow with her. She was in white. There were pearls and there were flowers and the long lacy veil, but all defied description when crowned with her look of anticipation and faith.

Mamá smiled on them all. "You girls look like a garden of lovely flowers."

Claudio sat in the second pew, Paul on one side, Mercedes on the other. He would have preferred a seat in the back of the church, one where he could gaze with complete intensity and anonymity. But he was family, and besides, Mercedes would not have understood. She squeezed his hand when her grandfather handed Aunt Trini over to her new husband. She wondered why he was looking at the bridesmaids, instead of at the bride and groom. Fathers were so weird sometimes!

When it came time for BOB to say his vows, he looked into Trini's eyes and tears filled his own. Though loud enough to hear, his voice was shaking. His head ducked once. He touched his mouth with the back of his hand and completely broke down. Trini gently laid her hand upon his back and put her head close to his. Together they said each other's vows, a poignant example of the helpmates they intended to be to one another.

Mamá turned at the end of the ceremony, to watch her lovely and triumphant third daughter sail down the aisle on the arm of her husband. She wiped her eyes and noticed her son-in-law, both sons-in-law, watching the bridesmaids that followed. Both seemed transfixed, each by only one girl. Mamá used her handkerchief to smother a tiny gasp.

She would not have predicted Claudio's stare.

The girls who looked like flowers wept throughout the ceremony. Afterwards, they gathered in the ladies room to repair the damage, Modesta commenting, "I didn't know I was going to cry!"

"I never know when anyone's going to cry," said Candelaria.

"Weddings always make me cry," laughed María Elena.

"Soft hearts were not made for makeup." Modesta was dabbing her face in the mirror.

"Sure they were!" Candelaria applied more lipstick. "We're probably their best customers."

The reception was close by, in a place called The Camelot, a rambling stone restaurant that might have been quite popular at one time and now barely sustained itself as a reception hall. It had a medieval air. Trini and BOB had liked the name.

Teb was well-acquainted with the bartenders at The Camelot and easily slipped into the crowd through the kitchen.

Just what do you think you're doing? the voice in his head said, when he was safely in the hall.

"Don't worry. I'm just looking. I won't stay to eat or anything crazy like that. One look won't hurt."

Oh, won't it? the voice sneered.

Modesta was the first to spot the intruder. "Okay. You do look ravishing in a tux," she conceded, hands planted on her hips.

"You gonna give me up?" he murmured. He raised his eyes to her face just in time. Only a daring woman with a perfect figure could wear a gown so sheer.

She shook her head. "I have a strange sympathy for the lovelorn."

"Ah, isn't this where you confess to having 'been there' yourself?"

She laughed. "Dance with me. We'll see if we can't shake her up!"

"I was trying to be incognito."

"You're safe with me."

"Somehow I doubt that..."

They twirled around the dance floor for a few songs. When Teb clutched her to himself, rather easily he thought, he asked, "And whom else are we doing this for?"

Modesta looked over his shoulder. "I have no idea what you're talking about."

"C'mon. I'm dancing to make María Elena jealous and you're dancing to make...?"

Modesta tossed her head, her neck incredibly long and smooth. "Don't be silly. I'm just helping you."

"My mistake," Teb laughed. "Charity begins at home?"

She gave him an arch look. "Anyone ever tell you, you talk too much?"

"No."

María Elena stared. It couldn't be! What was he doing here? She backed up and found herself on the balcony. The night air cooled her face. And what was Modesta doing, dancing with him? She looked over the stone railing. If the ground weren't so far away, she might have considered jumping.

"María Elena? Are you all right?"

She turned and automatically gave him a smile. "Oh, Claudio! Yes. Yes, I'm fine."

He cocked his head. "You don't look fine. You look like you just saw a ghost."

"No, no." She laughed. "These were real people, all right. No ghosts. Nope."

He looked quizzical.

María Elena took a deep breath. "Claudio, did you see Modesta on the dance floor?"

He smiled. "Yes, of course. Your sister is hard to miss."

"And her partner?"

"Oh, isn't that the fellow from your restaurant? I thought you must have invited him. No?"

"No! I pretty much did the opposite of that. I told him in no uncertain terms..."

"Ah. I see."

"See? See what?"

He chuckled. "Another man falls for the Méndez charm, to his peril."

She blushed. Very low she said, "Claudio, I swear I did nothing to lead him on."

She looked sincerely distressed. His face softened. "You know, your sister is probably just trying to get you two together. She has good intentions."

María Elena shook her head. "She knows I don't want that."

"Then," he said slowly, "perhaps instead of hiding, we should be on that dance floor."

María Elena bit her lip. This was a bold move for a man who kept to himself so much. His kindness touched her. She looked into his eyes and for the first time caught a glimpse of the man Adela had seen.

"María Elena," Claudio went on, in formal tones, "may I have this dance?" He bowed low and held out his arm.

"Yes," was all she said, but she took his arm and when he pressed her body to his, she did not pull back.

"Now, there is something I had not imagined!" Mamá was sitting at a table with Papá, sipping a glass of wine.

He looked in the direction of her gaze. "No?" was his mild response.

"Oh, and I suppose you had?"

He smiled. "I wished to keep the boy in the family, yes. And they seem well-suited to one another." He covered Mamá's small hand with his rough one. "And it is a good tradition. It often works out well for all."

She blushed.

Manuel coughed. "María," he said slowly, "you have no regrets, do you? I was so...confused, for a time." He squeezed her hand. "I made you wait."

"*Querida*," she interrupted him, "I have loved you since the day you and Oziel taught your uncle's donkey to throw him." She laughed at the memory and then looked wistful.

"What is it, Love?"

"You have given me more happiness than I dared imagine. I only..." Her soft voice grew softer. "I know it's selfish, but I did not wish to be a second choice."

"Oh, Love, you were never a second choice. You were a second chance, a precious miracle."

Carlos and Paul stood at the bar watching the dancers. "So," Paul said, "no starlet? No...what did you call her? Continuity girl?"

"Ha! Turned out she wasn't the one."

"Not consistent?"

"Too consistent. A consistency I didn't like."

Paul frowned. "You mean, like, texture? Too rough?"

"Not at all," Carlos barked. "More like, too smooth!"

"Slippery?"

"Yes, and sticky too."

"Okay, I must be drunk. I have no idea what we're talking about." Paul laughed and Carlos joined in.

"You know, Paul, I have to say you're good at keeping up."

"And keeping up with a Méndez is no joke, my friend. That's probably why Modesta finally agreed to marry me."

Carlos nodded. "Say, speaking of the ball and chain, who's she dancing with out there?"

Paul squinted in the direction of the dance floor.

"Huh. Beats me. But if he doesn't let go in about ten seconds I'm gonna have to make him..."

Carlos nodded and loosened his tie. "I'll help."

"Okay, all you love birds! Time to heat things up!" The bandleader lifted a trumpet and whipped the tempo into a frenzy of Latin samba.

A very pregnant Candelaria was pulling Nunzio to his feet. "Oh, you love this one!" she said. He laughed, nodded and rose slowly.

"Not too fast now, Candela," he cautioned.

She giggled. "I'll go easy on you, Dear, don't worry."

Modesta wiggled closer to her own partner. "Are you game, Esteban?"

A short quick nod and three hard twirls later, Teb said, "See if you can follow."

Nearby, Claudio and María Elena were moving quickly, smoothly, like they'd been dancing together forever. María Elena's hair came loose and she tossed her head to get it all behind her. Modesta's eyes narrowed. She gyrated so seductively, Teb had a hard time remembering they were only dancing.

Then Paul strode onto the floor. He tapped Teb on the shoulder. Hard. "Ow!" Teb stopped dancing. "Oh, hey, Man. Cutting?"

"You could say that," Paul replied. He swayed only slightly before crashing his fist into Teb's face.

The music stopped. The crowd gasped. Claudio pushed María Elena behind him and circled her with his arms.

"Stay away from my wife!" Paul growled. Modesta was frozen with surprise. He took her arm and, without speaking, led her away.

Carlos stood smiling at everyone, only a little disappointed that Paul hadn't needed his help after all.

On the other side of the dance floor, Nunzio and Candelaria paused. Nunzio grinned. "Well, it's about time. He had it coming!"

"You mean, she had it coming!" Candelaria answered.

"Who, my sister?"

"Absolutely! Are you blind? All she really needed was a man. And now," Candelaria crossed her arms decidedly. "She has one."

Carlos pulled Teb to his feet. He steered him to the door as the music started up again. He couldn't help pitying him. "You have to know how to play the game, man, before you jump in with both feet!"

Teb took the handkerchief he offered and pressed it to his bloody nose. "What the hell are you talking about?"

Carlos saw Nunzio approaching from the corner of his eye. "And you're just about out of time. Too bad!" Carlos pushed the door open. "Okay, Buddy, quickly then, number one – you're not gonna make anyone feel sorry for you, dancing with the hottest chick at the party. Two – you can't make a girl jealous, dancing with her older married sister. And three – listen up now, this is vital – the Méndez family sticks together. We're like...the Knights of the Round Table or something. You can't break in or sneak in, you have to be invited." With that he closed the door on hapless Teb.

Outside, on the same tiny stone balcony where María Elena and Claudio had spoken, an argument was taking place.

"Apologize? To whom? For what? I didn't do anything!" Modesta stamped her foot.

Paul's eyes were steely, his voice tight. "Didn't do anything? You little fool! You did so many things. I won't even take the time to list them. You blunder along, expecting everyone to just accept it. 'Oh, that's our Modesta! She's so beautiful. You must forgive her! Poor Modesta! So heartsick!' Well, it's time, Modesta," he spat her name, "for you to think of others for a change!"

Her mind had stopped at the word heartsick. Did he know? "Paul..." she put her hand on his arm, but he shook it off.

"This is where it ends," he snapped.

She suddenly felt sick. What if they were all laughing at her? Had even Paul had enough? He faced a breeze, his sandy curls blown back from his brow. She'd never seen his eyes so blue, his jaw so set. He looked like he did when they first dated, when he dared other men to flirt with her. Confident and self-possessed. She had forgotten how attractive he could be.

"I'm sorry, Paul," she whispered. "I didn't mean for this to..."

"Don't apologize to me. Go find your sister. You've done your best to ruin her day."

"Trinidad?" He only glared at her. She adjusted her dress. "Fine! Let's go." She waited for him to offer his arm. "Aren't you coming?"

"No." He walked back to the bar. He'd never said no to his wife before.

"Jack Daniels. Straight up."

"Whoa." Carlos clapped his brother-in-law on the back. "Hard stuff, huh?"

Paul nodded. "But not as hard as I thought. You know, I was always afraid of upsetting your sister. I gave in to everything. But that doesn't work, does it?"

"Nah." Carlos motioned to the bartender to give him the same. "They want what they can't have, man, not what they can!"

"I don't know...I think Modesta might not want what she's already had." Paul smiled grimly. "¡Salud!"

They drank.

"Now what are we supposed to do?" María Elena was still standing behind Claudio. She was noticing his broad shoulders, the way cologne smelled only manlier on him.

"Better act natural." He chuckled. "Keep dancing."

He turned and quickly put his arms around her. They were playing a slow song.

María Elena giggled. "Claudio, you're a trooper."

"I've been in the family for a long time now. One learns."

"That you never know what you're going to get with a Méndez?"

"That you'll never get what you expect. You'll get a whole lot more."

She blushed, looked over his shoulder at the other couples dancing. "Was Adela like that?"

"Ah, Adelina was very much like that! And so is Mercedes." He paused. "And so are you." He cleared his throat. "I understand you're graduating early. All that studying paid off."

María Elena smiled. "I guess. That was the plan anyway."

"And what next? Graduate school or a job?"

"Ha! You sound like an interviewer, or an adviser, or a father."

"Well, I am a father."

"I'd like to continue my education, yes, and then maybe find a teaching position while I write."

He nodded as she spoke. "Very good."

"Do you think so?" She was surprised to discover that she cared what he thought.

"Yes! One needs a great deal of understanding to be a powerful writer. Only certain people, no matter how gifted, are able to achieve it."

"I see. You know, you're awfully smart. Did you ever think about writing?"

"Not really. I read a lot. I think. I raise my daughter. That's enough. Your sister used to encourage me to express myself, but it was mostly wishful thinking."

"Really? Adela wanted you to write?"

"She found a poem that I wrote in high school – high school, María Elena! Can you believe it?" He laughed and laughed. She laughed too. She almost said, "I'd like to see that", but stopped herself just in time.

"Oh, dear, it's ended."

"Yes, well, that was a long time ago. Do you still play the oboe?"

"No, no, I mean the music's stopped."

"Oh. How long do you suppose we've been dancing to empty air? Perhaps if we don't stop, nobody will notice."

She smiled. Oh, someone was going to notice, all right! "Claudio," she whispered, "let's get something to drink."

"Well, that didn't go very well, did it?" Trini was looking right at her sister. Modesta didn't flinch.

"I have no idea what you're talking about, but I would like to apologize for any responsibility that I may have had in the skirmish!"

"That's your apology?" Trini burst into a laugh. "Any responsibility? How about all of it? You're such an idiot sometimes!"

"Well! No need to call names!"

"And what made you think it would work? Why did you have to drag a total stranger into it? And where in God's name did you find that dress? I know I said I only wanted you guys in the same color, but Strippers-R-Us?"

"It's designer!"

"It's barely there!" Trini smoothed her hair. They were primping in the ladies room. Trini was radiant with her hair all in tight little curls and her cheeks glowing. Modesta was still sleek and smooth. Trini pressed lipstick to her upper lip. "Sorry. It's beautiful, really. Now, who exactly were you trying to make jealous?"

"No one. You know." Modesta cringed.

"Poor Teb!"

"Yes, well, poor Teb showed up on his own. I had nothing to do with that! He'll just have to work a little harder."

"Are you kidding? He doesn't have a chance anymore."

"What do you mean?" Modesta leaned back on the counter. She could feel sweat beading on her brow.

"Didn't you see? There's no way he can compete with our Claudio."

"With our Claudio?" Modesta hurried back out to the party and looked around. Where was everyone? Oh, there, by the bar! Carlos, BOB, Paul, Nunzio and Candelaria, and Claudio and María Elena! They were standing together, laughing, drinking, celebrating. She saw how close Claudio and María Elena were. She saw the way he gazed at her when he thought no one was looking. "I've never seen him look like that," she murmured.

"Sure you have," Trini answered behind her.

"No. He never even looked at me that way!
When?"

"Just before he asked Adela out." Modesta bit
her lip. "Time to let him go, Mo." Trini raised her
arm to put it around her sister's shoulders and
then changed her mind and dropped it. They
were silent for a while.

Finally Modesta cleared her throat. "You
know, it's funny. I had forgotten how tall my
husband is. Good looking, too. I'm standing this
close to him, and he's not even looking at me."

"Ha. That's got to be a first."

BOB waved the two over.

"C'mon. Let's join them!"

"You go. He means you." Modesta turned her
back on her family and headed for the balcony.
She couldn't see Paul watching her.

"Hey, man," BOB urged, "Go after her. You
know you want to."

"Doesn't work that way, my friend. She has
to come after me." Paul smiled and turned the
other way.

Trini refused to throw her bouquet. She didn't
want the chicken dance or the Hokey Pokey
either. Her wedding would be traditional in some
ways, but not all. There were fancy jars of
painted stones on each table for centerpieces.
And the women's favors were all tubes of red
lipstick tied in lace, fitting mementoes of her
relationship with BOB.

By midnight, the Camelot was ready to close.
Trini and BOB piled into his car, festooned with
crepe paper and tin cans. They rode off into the

night. Trini was very anxious. They hadn't made love since that one time, long ago.

"BOB," she said, "you won't believe this, but I'm actually nervous."

He squeezed her hand. "I know."

"You know?"

"Yes." He smiled at the darkened road. "It's my present, my wedding present to you."

"Anxiety?"

"A proper wedding night."

"You mean...?"

He nodded. "Do you think I wanted to wait? Think there weren't plenty of times when I said to myself, 'C'mon you idiot! She wants to do it! It would reassure her! It would be a good thing!'"

"But you never said anything!"

"No. We wouldn't have had this night, then, would we?"

Trini laughed. "You really are my knight in shining armor, sometimes, you know that?"

Modesta was by a window, pretending to drink, watching her husband at the bar. He was handsome, vigorous; he would have been so happy with someone else! She tilted her head, sipped some more, and for the first time, she wondered why he stayed. The secret she was sure she had been keeping, did everyone know it? Even Paul? And then he turned and looked right at her. Modesta lifted her chin. She thought he would come over, but he didn't. Instead, he just kept staring, and with his stare, he drew her to himself.

"Paul."

"Modesta."

"You know, you haven't protected my honor in a long, long time."

"On the contrary. We're still married, aren't we?"

"Ah! That's why you stayed."

He smiled at his drink, shook his head. "No."

"I've been watching you," Modesta pointed to her window, "From over there. You're very handsome."

He shrugged. "I don't put so much stock in looks."

Modesta laughed. "Of course you do!" She tossed her head.

Paul grabbed her arms. "You little idiot! You think that's why I'm here?"

Modesta blushed. She tried to look away, but could not. "Well, that or some archaic honor system that won't let you break a vow."

"Archaic what?" He laughed, but bitterly. "You've given me every reason in the world to 'break a vow,' but I did vow to love you until death and goddamn it, I still do, no matter what. That doesn't mean I'll stay to suffer your ingratitude, however."

"Paul..."

He let go of her. "Why are you still here? If I'm not the man you want; what are you doing with me?"

"Paul, you, I mean..." Modesta stammered. She didn't know what to do with honesty, not after so many years of pretending.

"You can't even answer me." He threw back the rest of his whiskey.

"I can, but it's not flattering, to me or to you either." Modesta took one of Paul's hands. She turned it over. Large, manicured, long fingers with blond hairs. She loved his hands; she always had. She thought back to the day they met. She'd seen him in the office only once and that's all it took. Modesta whispered, "Oh Paul, I keep thinking if I stay it might come back."

"What might?"

"That lovely exciting feeling that the world was made just for us! My youth, and yours, and our pure delight in belonging to each other."

"You are so blind!"

"I am?"

"It's all still here." He touched his heart. "And here." He laid his hand on her heart now and she covered it with her own. "Mo, you don't love him. You only miss your youth."

She would have cried if his mouth hadn't been on hers.

María Elena and Mamá were wrapping a plate of cookies. Mercedes was helping. "Cucho would like these sugar cookies. They look like dog biscuits."

"Mercedes!" Mamá laughed. "Those are supposed to be crowns! For the wedding couple! You cannot feed wedding cookies to a dog!"

"But poor Cucho missed the whole wedding!" Mercedes pouted. "He should get something." She picked up a crown and bit into it. "Ugh! Not this though! Who made these cookies?"

Claudio came up behind her. "Your Aunt Mo did."

"Aunt Modesta should stick to *empanadas*!" They laughed.

"She's learning to stick, I think." Mamá nodded to where a few couples were still slow dancing, Modesta and Paul, Nunzio and Candelaria. The band had left already, and the club was playing a tape in an effort to get everyone else to leave.

Papá came over. "Come on, María!" He pulled Mamá onto the dance floor, ignoring her protests.

María Elena said, "They make a handsome couple."

Claudio looked thoughtful. "They do." He turned to María Elena. "Do you need a ride home tonight?"

"Hmm? A ride? Oh, no thanks. I'll just go home with Mamá and Dad," she nodded to her parents. "It's out of your way Claudio, and you have to get Mercedes to bed..."

"Of course, of course." He took her hand. "I'll say goodnight then. Thank you for keeping an eye on Mercedes."

"Oh, Claudio, she's a pleasure. You know, you should get out more. Go dancing. You're really very good at it."

He chuckled. "Come, Mercedes. Let's find your Aunt Trini and Uncle BOB."

María Elena quit her job on Monday. She enrolled in a graduate program at the University and sighed with resignation. She would have to find a job somewhere. Two more years to live with her parents!

Mamá invited Mercedes over often. She used the excuse that Mercedes needed a woman's influence. They cooked together, sewed. She even taught the child how to use the washing machine. "Mamá," María Elena said one day, "Mercedes is lucky. Do you remember teaching us to do laundry with your old wringer washer? It was so long ago. That old machine would be obsolete now!"

"No matter," Mamá replied. "Learning is never a mistake. You of all people should know that."

When Claudio came to fetch his daughter, Mamá always invited him to stay for supper, or coffee or a cookie. He always refused. Mamá never said anything until the day María Elena noticed.

"Mamá," María Elena asked one day, "why doesn't Claudio visit us anymore? We see more of Mercedes than we do of him!"

"Well, he is very busy. Working and keeping house and all!"

"Too busy to say hello?"

"Perhaps if you asked him..."

María Elena shrugged. "Okay."

But in the end, it was really her father who made the difference. That very day, when Claudio pulled up the long dirt driveway, Papá was in the barn, watching. He sauntered out, very casual like.

"Ah, Claudio!" he said, strolling over to the car. "How's she running?"

"The car? All right, I guess. I just came by to get Mercedes. How are you doing, Sir?" He shook his father-in-law's hand.

"Well, fine. Just fine! We don't see much of you anymore. Why not stay for dinner?"

Claudio looked off into the woods behind the barn. "Ah, no, I don't think so..."

"She misses you."

Claudio blushed. "What? Who?"

"María Elena. Ever since the wedding, you have been avoiding her, and avoiding her means avoiding us. You know, you cannot hide forever!"

"I don't know what you're talking about." But by his face, it was evident that he did.

"Come with me, Son. We need to talk." Papá led Claudio to a bench behind the barn. A lone blue jay was singing at the edge of the woods. The smell of fall was intoxicating. "You know, María was not my first wife."

"No, sir. I did not know that!"

"When I was a much younger man, I was married to her sister, Rafaela. We were only married a year when she died."

"Ah."

"I know how hard it is. At first, you think you never will recover from your broken heart and then when you do, it is unseemly that you should love so wholeheartedly again! You are afraid it somehow dishonors the love you bore."

Claudio hung his head.

"But, it was the custom at that time, in that place, to marry the next youngest sister."

"And that was Mamá?"

Papá nodded. "That was my María. And now, I cannot imagine life without her. Rafaela and I had no children, but had we, Mamá would have been the best of mothers to them. She is a dear companion and if I am perfectly honest, I will admit that I do not love her less than her sister. In fact, I believe I love her more."

"But we don't follow that custom any longer..."

"It was a good tradition. It saved a family. It kept a family intact. It healed broken hearts." Papá stood and touched Claudio on the shoulder. "María Elena wonders why she hasn't seen you since the wedding. Think about it."

A little while later Claudio appeared at the kitchen door. "Ah, Mamá," he called. "Something smells good! What's for supper? May I stay?"

For The Milagros
Of Life, Of Faith

Nearly as strong as she was before her illness, María pinned the last sheet to the line and lifted the basket to her hip. The wind blew little tendrils of hair from her face. Without thinking, she smiled.

"Ah," Mamá took the basket from her. "You got all the wash hung? You are such a help! Now, go sit down. Relax!"

"I'm fine, Mamá," she said, surprised that she meant it. "I'll feed the goat for you," and off she went.

Mamá shook her head at María's bare feet, her lovely figure hurrying away to the barn. "That boy is a fool. The Lord would not want this!" And with a harrumph, she stalked back to the house.

María's father was in the barn. He was currying the old horse, one hand on her white back, the other making long strokes with the brush. María watched as the horse stood, quivering with pleasure. "Her coat still has a sheen to it as though she were much younger. You take good care of her, Papá."

Her father smiled and continued brushing. "Neva is a good girl." He patted her side. "She does all I ask. Uncomplaining. It was hard on her when Paloma was sold, but, one has to do the difficult task sometimes." He turned to look at his daughter, his eyes narrowing. "Mamá wants to ride out to make a visit today."

"Of course." María looked down. She wiggled her toes on the dirt floor of the barn.

"And you?"

"Oh, no. I'll walk. I always do." She smiled suddenly at her father and he grinned back.

"Don't wait too long to go then. It's going to get hot."

"I'll just feed the goat first." She patted old Neva on her way to the goat. Her father kept his smile as he finished brushing the horse.

María kicked off her shoes and knelt in the grass. With one hand she fingered her rosary beads and with the other, she pulled a weed from the flowers that caressed her sister's headstone. She frowned as she prayed, examining the flowers, the stone. All would be perfect by the time her mother got there. When she had finished tidying up the grave, María sat back on her heels. "Rafaela," she murmured, "you would have been twenty-three." She closed her eyes and softly sang:

> *This is the morning song that King David*
> *sang*
> *Because today is your saint's day we're*

singing it for you
Wake up, my dear, wake up, look it is
already dawn

Her voice broke. Rafaela never woke with the dawn! Oh, how María missed her sweet laughter, her cheerful humming as she did her chores. She shook herself, cleared her throat. Her sister had always loved the next lines of the song:

The birds are already singing and the moon
has set
How lovely is the morning in which I come to
greet you
We all came with joy and pleasure to
congratulate you
The morning is coming now, the sun is
giving us its light
Get up in the morning, look it is already
dawn.

Her eyes filled with tears as she thought of all the mornings left to come, with no sweet Rafaela to tease and coax from her bed. Her voice wavered on:

The day you were born all the flowers were
born
On the baptismal font the nightingales
sang –

María stopped again, pressed her eyes closed, overcome for a moment, and a voice she recognized, deep and sweet, bravely picked up the tune:

I would like to be the sunshine to enter
through your window

*to wish you good morning while you're lying
in your bed
I would like to be a Saint John, I would like
to be a Saint Peter
To sing to you with the music of heaven
Of the stars in the sky I have to lower two
for you
One with which to greet you and the other to
wish you goodbye.*

His voice lingered over the last word. She waited, but there was no sob, only a sigh. María held her breath. She couldn't move, not even to open her eyes, until she felt his hand upon her shoulder. Only then was she brave enough to lift her lids a little and when the hand moved to her chin, tilted her face to his, her eyes flew open wide. He said, "I knew you would be here."

María couldn't speak.

"Can you forgive me?"

With a sinking heart she whispered, "For what?"

"For making you wait so long."

She nearly fainted. Did he really say that?

He took her hands, drew her to her feet. "It is fitting that I ask you here, in front of her, on this day of all days."

Oh, God was good! María trembled. "A present to her?" she murmured.

Manuel shook his head. "She was a gift to me. I don't know why our Lord is blessing me so twice, but you are a gift as well. Rafaela would approve. She always kept you with us, didn't she?"

María nodded.

"She knew one day you would be mine." He raised his eyebrows and María quickly nodded.

"And you mine, Love."

He clasped her to his heart, a heart that finally began to make sense of love and loss, one's journey to heaven and the gift of heaven on earth. A bird landed on Rafaela's headstone, a cardinal, her favorite. It chirped gleefully. Manuel and María smiled. "You see," he said, "she does approve." He waved his arm about them, "All of nature smiles upon us."

María nodded. "God approves."

Your Love-Braced Cornerstone

"Why must you and your husband go away?"

María looked down to keep from smiling. Her husband. Manuel belonged to her and she to him. The wonder of this was like the first glimmer of sun on a winter morning, or the time she and her sister rode the carousel at the Texas state fair, or her first taste of ice cream. "You know, Mamá. Manuel has a job. Teaching at a high school in Pennsylvania. It will be exciting to see what the North is like."

Her mother crossed herself. "*El Norte.*" She shook her head.

"Ah," María's father stepped into the room bringing the scent of the outdoors and a slight fragrance of gasoline with him. "The car is ready. Your oil is changed and all fluids are full." He bowed to his younger daughter before turning to the kitchen to wash his hands.

"You're driving so far! It will take hours, days," her mother lamented.

"They have plenty of time." Father returned, drying his hands. "Pennsylvania – a good place to start a family." He kept drying. María waited to hear his next words, sure that they would be either a blessing or a warning. She did not anticipate a question. "Do you know, María, why they call Pennsylvania the Keystone State?"

"No." She knit her brow.

"Ah." He turned to hang his carefully folded hand towel on the sink.

Mamá stepped briskly to the sink and re-hung the very straight towel. "And has Manuel always wanted to go north?"

María shook her head. "I don't think so, not always. He told me his studies made him wish to see more of the world. History, geography, it made him curious."

"Ah, *sí*." Her father nodded.

"What is it, Father?"

"So," her mother crossed her arms, "it isn't that Falfurrias has become too small, too boring for a great thinker like Manuel?"

"Mother, Manuel wouldn't make a decision this important, or any decision, for that matter, out of pride!" María walked over to where her father stood looking out the kitchen door. The sun was setting and its red and orange light made the little room glow.

"María," he asked, "what did you fix for supper tonight?"

"For supper? Beans, tortillas, a little beef. Why, Father?"

He turned, faced his daughter and asked more sternly, "And where are your shoes?"

"Oh. Ah, I think they're in the bedroom closet. Or maybe under the bed. I'm not sure. I didn't bother with them today." She moved behind a chair and tried to hide her bare feet.

"Your mother-in-law must be shocked at such peasant ways!"

She tried hard not to laugh.

María's father regarded his beautiful young daughter, clad in a simple cotton dress, her hair in braids, feet bare. He tried to picture her in a fancy kitchen in Pittsburgh, Pennsylvania, which he was sure was very modern. *They say the sky there is black with smoke because of the steel mills, the sun a faint glimmer.* He shook his head, wondering how his innocent, nature loving child would fare, so far away from all she loved.

Manuel entered with a knock at the door, his hat in his hand. María spun around on her toes and greeted him, her face alight with joy. *Well, perhaps not so far from all she loved,* Father conceded.

Manuel hugged his wife and then quietly greeted his in-laws. "Good evening, good evening. May I steal my wife back now? We have a good deal of packing left to finish."

"Manuel," María's father said slowly, "if she is your wife you are not stealing, you know."

"Ah, *sí*," he stammered. "You understand. I only hope you also understand why I must take her so far away."

"And from Rafaela too!" Mamá pressed her handkerchief against her mouth. "Is it really necessary?"

Manuel blushed at the sound of his first wife's name, may she rest in peace. Then he got a steely look in his eye and answered evenly, "We will take our memories and the love we bear for our family with us. That much is always packed."

María swallowed hard, but she smiled up at Manuel. He was her hero, to the last.

Manuel continued, "Please understand, *Mamá Flaca, Padre*, we believe it best to take the opportunity the Lord has placed before us. We don't wish to be far from you, but one has to take risks sometimes."

María's father nodded. "Find the answer to my question, María! It will answer your question as well."

Manuel and María were home in no time, back in the rooms that Manuel had shared with Rafaela. "María," Manuel said as he held the door open, "what question did you ask your father?"

"Manuel, I didn't ask him anything. He knew I wanted to know what he thought of our move. That must be the question he was referring to."

"Ah. And what was his question?"

"He asked me if I knew why they call Pennsylvania the Keystone State."

Manuel laughed.

"Do you know?"

"It's not that, it's just – your father is very wise. I think I'll miss him more than I will mine."

"We'll write often," María said staunchly. "And besides, you'll be so busy you won't even have time to miss them." She added under her breath, "Nor will I."

The next day María was on her way to her cousin's house, to bid Encarnación farewell and even though the walk was short, she grew faint only halfway there. As she passed the library on her way, she decided to rest there. The tiny worn building did not offer much comfort, but it did contain information, a shiny set of encyclopedias, the spines of the books ramrod stiff. María stood in front of them thoughtfully, then slowly pulled out the volume showing a golden letter P. María was somewhat distracted by the grandness of Philadelphia and Pittsburgh, before she flipped to the front of the book to find Pennsylvania, the Keystone State:

The Keystone State

A keystone is a central wedge in an arch that locks all other pieces of an arch in place. It is the part of an arch that all other parts depend upon.

Pennsylvania's popular nickname, "The Keystone State," refers to this necessary element. Like most nicknames, it Is not known, for certain, where this name originated, but there are a few interesting thoughts about how this nickname came to be. They are all based on the theme of the necessity of a keystone in a supporting structure.

In the vote for independence, nine delegates to the Continental Congress were from the Commonwealth of Pennsylvania. It's said that the Pennsylvania delegation was split; four for independence and four against. The deciding vote fell to John Morton...who voted for independence. Pennsylvania's vote for independence was noted as the keystone vote; the supporting vote for a new government.

When the government was moved to Washington, D.C., a bridge was built over Rock Creek to Georgetown. This bridge was the Pennsylvania Avenue Bridge. Pennsylvania's initials were carved into the "keystone" of the arch supporting the bridge.

Another explanation has it that Pennsylvania's geographic location, among the original thirteen colonies, was the basis for this nickname.

Though the nickname's origin is unknown, it's certain that it was in use around, or shortly after, 1800. It's reported that Pennsylvania was toasted as "...the keystone of the federal union" at a Republican presidential victory rally for Thomas Jefferson in 1802. Regardless of its origin, the nickname has come to represent Pennsylvania's geographic, economic, social and political impact on development of the United States.[*]

María didn't get any farther than this before the warm air and the droning of an overhead fan began to make her nod. Why would her father care that she know Pennsylvania's history? She certainly didn't know much history about Falfurrias or Texas, for that matter. She rubbed her eyes and began again. A keystone was like a cornerstone, the central element of the foundation. Where had she heard this before, or something like it...?

[*] Source: www.netstate.com

The old church bell pealed. María glanced up at the clock on the wall. Time for noon Mass? She touched her stomach lightly and smiled. Her cousin would have lunch waiting, but perhaps first, she would pray.

As María crossed the street and entered the cool stone structure that always smelled of incense, she examined the arches surrounding her. She made out various keystones and studied how the other stones all pushed against them, thrusting upward as if to heaven and to – *yes, yes! That was it. He is the cornerstone.*

And this is why my father trusts in our decision to leave. With Jesus as our keystone, our cornerstone, it doesn't matter where we live. Our family will be fine and strong and we will make the world a better place no matter where we settle.

María stayed for the Mass and offered it as a blessing to all the family and friends they would leave behind and to the new family, the three of them, who were moving north. She trusted as her father did, that they were following the Lord. She hadn't told Manuel yet that they were traveling with a child, but she wasn't worried. As long as she and Manuel had their keystone and each other, they would live well, bearing all life's sorrows and rejoicing always in God's provident *milagros.*

Milagros

Heaven is
Your unfailing, all-knowing Love,
answer to whispered prayers.
Unbidden and authentic,
comfort of the outcast,
gracious Love appear.
Occupy the hollow;
cover our inadequacy;
forgive us the sin of loving one another too much.
Allow us to trust in Your greater plan for our welfare,
granting strength and patience to resist what is not ours
and the courage to act upon our most precious convictions.
Wrapped in the innocent and candid faith of children,
our hope in You sustains.
Punctuate our ordinary time
with Your guiding candle,
luminous in lush and desert,
relentless miracle.
Grace cup to the dying,
wisdom to the living;
may we be made worthy
of Your infinite clemency,
discovering Holy Treasure
in the mercy we bestow.
Give us courage.
Entrust our days and nights To You
that in pursuit of heaven's honor
we may celebrate, ever grateful
for the milagros of life, of faith —
Your love-braced cornerstone.

About the Author

Tess Almendárez Lojacono is a writer, business owner and a teacher. Her company, Fine Art Miracles, seeks to accomplish two goals: 1) to bring attention to the underserved through fine art education and 2) to embrace humanity in the elucidation of common experiences and emotions. She has a BFA from Carnegie Mellon University. *International Family Magazine* has named her Editor of its Latin Families Column, where you can find her stories, along with the work of other Latin writers. Tess' poems and stories have appeared in *OffCourse*, a literary journal, in *The Cortland Review, Flash Fiction Online, St. María's Messenger, Falling Star Magazine, The Shine Journal, A Fly In Amber, Joyful!, Etchings Magazine, Envoy Magazine* and *Words and Images*.

Other Books
from
Laughing Cactus Press
imprint of
Silver Boomer Books

Poetry Floats
New and selected Philosophy-lite
by Jim Wilson
August, 2009

Bluebonnets, Boots and Buffalo Bones
by Sheryl L. Nelms
September, 2009

not so GRIMM
gentle fables and cautionary tales
by Becky Haigler
November, 2009

Three Thousand Doors
by Karen Elaine Greene
August, 2010

From Silver Boomer Books:

Silver Boomers
prose and poetry by and about baby boomers
March, 2008

Freckles to Wrinkles
August, 2008

This Path
September, 2009

Song of County Roads
by Ginny Greene
September, 2009

From the Porch Swing – memories of our grandparents
July, 2010

Flashlight Memories
coming February, 2011

From Eagle Wings Press, imprint of Silver Boomer Books:

Slender Steps to Sanity – Twelve-Step Notes of Hope
by OAStepper, Compulsive Overeater
May, 2009

Writing Toward the Light – A Grief Journey
by Laura Flett
July, 2009

A Time for Verse
poetic ponderings on Ecclesiastes
by Barbara B. Rollins
December, 2009

Survived to Love
by Ed H
August, 2010

White Elephants
by Chynna T. Laird
Febuary, 2011

226547LV00003B/73/P

9 780982 624340